Light of the Sea

Ancient Rome from a sailor's point of view.

Historical fiction in a novel format.

By

Captain Clair

Light of the Sea

ISBN: 978-0-615-29803-0

Printed in the United States of America

Refreshing Leaders Publishing
P.O. Box 241
East Earl, PA 17519
1-877-732-2278
www.refreshingleaders.com
captainclair@refreshingleaders.com

"Scripture taken from HOLY BIBLE, NEW INTERNATIONAL
VERSION®. Copyright © 1973, 1978, 1984 by International
Bible Society. Used by permission of Zondervan Publishing
House."

Cover Design: Peri Poloni-Gabriel, Knockout Design,
www.knockoutbooks.com

Editor: Marjorie Spang

Table of Contents

Chapter 1

Desperation Aboard Shanesse

The wind screamed through the rigging like a tortured animal meeting its death. The ever-increasing waves were defiant and unpredictable, intent on coming aboard. The intrusive seas that crashed on deck foamed and churned, angrily testing every lug and fastener for strength. Then the receding water surged and swirled as it diligently challenged the joints and seams, trying to gain access. The battle raged between man and sea. The sea furiously attempted to claim Shanesse as her own and the men defended her with their lives. In a desperate reach for a short reprieve, they set their course for the leeward of Claudia Island.

Shanesse flew the Alexandrian flag and was named after the eldest daughter of the queen. She was a fine vessel, built to the most exacting standards of any modern day ship. With an expert crew, not a sailor aboard had less than three years at sea, she was certified to carry precious cargo from every major port in the world. More impressively, she had earned the Gold Seal of Caesar himself. This meant that she could carry payroll from Rome in the form of gold and silver coins as well as other cargo so precious that no one but Captain Warnken knew of its contents. Oh, they understood its value alright, but that was something they just *knew*, speaking of it would reveal a seaman's inexperience. These men comprised one of the top crews in the world.

They had weathered some severe storms in the past and their outstanding abilities coupled with undaunted allegiance earned them Caesar's highest certification. Carrying dignitaries and other influential citizens, captain and crew were always prepared for the worst, willing to risk their very lives for the good of Shanesse, their passengers, and the precious cargo protected deep within her holds.

But things had gone terribly wrong. They sailed out of Myra, a city of Lycia many days ago with a cargo that they would not discuss, and nearly two hundred paying passengers. All that could be said was this: A few of the passengers were important enough, and the cargo valuable enough to Rome, that Captain Warnken was persuaded to sail right up against the winter weather window to complete the trip.

Because of contrary winds earlier in their trip, they had sailed with much difficulty just to get to Fair Havens. Having lost many valuable days, sailing on to Rome before the winter weather set in was out of the question. Fair Havens, however, was not suitable for wintering either, and having to protect their passengers and cargo through the winter months, they had no alternative but to move on.

After careful consideration, Captain Warnken chose the harbor in Phoenix which was just a short distance away on the same island of Crete. This harbor lay northeast to southwest and was suitable for wintering. Finding a good anchorage late in the season was a significant problem. Many smaller, less capable vessels would have prepared for winter weeks ago. Anticipating the harbor to be practically full by then, the sooner they could get there, the better chance they would have of securing Shanesse in a desirable location. She was a large elegant vessel and needed more room than some.

When Captain Warnken decided to sail out of Fair Havens that day, they knew it was a risk, but all aboard were eager to make the quick dash for Phoenix and secure the ship there. All except one, that is. One of the passengers, a prisoner being escorted to Rome by a detachment of soldiers, did not want to leave. Carrying prisoners was commonplace for them, as they were the transportation of choice when the centurions were anywhere near the coast. Both the sailors and centurions carried equally intense responsibility in their respective jobs. For those guarding the prisoners, the penalty was uncommonly severe if there was an escape. They would pay with their own lives when they stood to answer before Caesar. But while aboard Shanesse, the centurions were able to relax; escape or liberation by an ambush was not a concern for them at sea.

To everyone's consternation, the prisoner, who went by the name of Paul, had openly and boldly declared that the voyage would end in disaster with the total loss of the cargo. Those in charge, including Benjobo the owner, and Captain Warnken seemed to think that the prisoner was simply making a lot of noise, fearful of his ultimate demise as he was to stand trial before Caesar. Normally, mention of the loss of cargo while in any port would have caught the Captain's keen ear and instantly the crew would have gone on high alert, every sailor having his weapon of choice within easy reach. The crew clearly understood, the sea was not the only thing they had to protect their cargo from. Both at sea and in port it was well known that they would put their lives on the line to protect Shanesse, her passengers and her cargo. Few were the bands of raiders bold enough to challenge them. Shanesse and her crew had earned a fierce reputation over the years and were highly respected in ports of call all over the civilized world. Of those unfortunate enough to have challenged them for their cargo, few had lived to tell their story.

This man Paul seemed different from the other prisoners. He was disconcertingly confident for one thing, which no one could understand as he was not just any common prisoner, but one who was going on trial before Caesar himself. He had said that they would not only lose the cargo, but also Shanesse and their lives. Not because a band of outlaws would destroy the ship and steal the cargo, but he said that the weather was going to turn against them. At the time there was little concern among the crew; Paul did not know how capable Shanesse was. She was built to handle the roughest weather and Captain Warnken was unsurpassed in his leadership, with an experienced crew that would follow him to hell and back. Additionally, the reason that they had to leave Fair Havens was so that the weather did not overcome them, they could not winter there. But now, as they fought their way to the bow in the deafening scream of wind and rain, Paul's words seemed to echo in the wind and fight against their minds as aggressively as the waves fought against the ship. They began to believe that he had spoken an evil omen over them! Who was this Paul? In all their years at sea, and all the storms they had fought their way through, they had never experienced a storm such as this!

They had sailed from Fair Havens staying close to Crete with light seas and a soft south wind, but only hours later the wind picked up and turned directly against them. With a stiffening head wind and building seas, conditions rapidly deteriorated. Within another hour they could no longer hold their course so they turned and ran before the wind. For the next few hours the wind and waves continued to build. As expected, with the change in wind direction came very confused seas. The waves were running exceptionally steep and close together with a heavy opposing chop.

With the intensity of their situation escalating alarmingly, they secured their sails and ran under bare poles, only the small storm jibs remained in an effort to maintain steerage. Every sailor working top side had been ordered to wear body and soul lashings to keep the oil skins from blowing right off their bodies. Those were ropes tied around the sleeves and trouser legs, with multiple lashings around the waist and body. The work on deck had become so severe that they were limited to twenty minutes instead of the normal four hour shifts. The force of the storm required two men on the wheel at all times as it reacted violently to the forces of the churning sea. It would literally fling a man overboard if it spun free and caught on his arm or clothing. Shanesse was taking an incredible pounding as they ran before the wind, oscillating violently from forty degrees starboard through forty degrees to port. At the same time she was climbing up the steep back of a wave with her bow raised high above the crest. Then, with the wave acting as a fulcrum supporting her entire weight amidships, she moaned and creaked as the bow rotated into a down position. With the stern high above the water she roared down the face of the wave, plunging her bow deep into the trough, bringing a wall of water crashing on deck. Shivering her timbers, her decks awash with tons of foaming churning water, she could not stabilize between the waves because the trough was too small to settle in. Her bow struggled to rise, climbing the back of the next wave, but her stern was still supported by the last one, she groaned and creaked once more as her weight was now supported by bow and stern. Surely another ship would have succumbed to the excruciating forces!

Capt. Warnken boomed, "All hands on deck!" as they neared the small remote island of Claudia. A difficult reach to say the least, but having struggled desperately they arrived to the leeward of the island. The waves were calmer now but their time was fleeting. Capt. Warnken continued, "We have to take full advantage of every second in these protected waters."

He ordered twenty sailors to secure the skiff on deck, which they accomplished with much difficulty, and another team to retrieve the storm jibs, in order to slow the ship and buy as much time as possible. Capt. Warnken then made the obvious choice, calling Jag, Ulray, Mecho and Nassor, the ship's finest and most reliable officers and laid out a very desperate plan. It went undeclared, but every sailor aboard knew that when ship and crew faced great peril, the four of them would be chosen to deal with the problem. Struggling to keep from being blasted overboard by the incredible swirling leeward winds the four officers made their way to the bow with their teams. The task at hand was to secure ropes under the distressed vessel to keep her from breaking up.

Nassor climbed out the bowsprit and worked one end of the rope around the headstay and Mecho secured weights on each section of rope just a bit wider than her beam. Ulray and Jag worked them aft, one man starboard and one port. They had strategically placed the ropes and had passed them off to their teams who secured them to multiple cleats. Other crew members were mending the netting that was in place along the railing, which was there to strain out sailors and keep them from washing overboard if they should lose their footing as a wave crashed over the deck. Still others were checking that everything on deck was secure. Some large barrels had worked themselves loose earlier and were in danger of going awash. Something as simple as a barrel of drinking water could break equipment or worse, kill a sailor if it broke free.

In a short time the crew was forced to raise a sail and escape the vacuum created on the leeward side of the island. The fierce driving rain felt like arrows striking any exposed skin, and it was nearly impossible for them to see. They had been weathering this brutal storm for a full day, and all feared for the survival of Shanesse and those aboard her. Knowing Captain Warnken so well, his officers could sense his deep concern. Their considerable experience alerted them to his apprehension because, in all their years at sea, they had never been ordered to put ropes under the ship to keep her from breaking up. Nassor wondered if Capt. had ever felt this frightened before. This certainly was a last ditch effort, but it was an ingenious idea. Nassor reassured himself, "If anyone can get us through this storm, it's Capt. Warnken!"

With the ropes secure, they were nearly out of time. Returning to the aft deck by the wheel they could hear the Captain shouting orders.

"Jag, Ulray, Mecho and Nassor, set our smallest storm sail, we need to maneuver out of here, be careful!" Nassor was only two paces away and could scarcely hear the orders as his words seemed to be whisked away by the wind. Under normal circumstances his imposing voice could be clearly heard at the far end of the ship but now, barely hearing his command, Nassor could clearly sense the urgency of the situation. Nassor and Jag went to starboard and Ulray and Mecho to port. Climbing up the forward ratlines ("rattlin's," small pieces of rope tied between the shrouds, forming a ladder) and hanging on for their lives they worked to secure the sail to the lower yard. Using only hand signs to communicate, since words could not be heard, Mecho completed the last loop and held out his hand to signal that he was ready on the far port side. At that moment an exceptionally strong gust of wind hit him, violently jerking his right foot free and leaving him with only his left hand and left leg wrapped around the yard arm. The furled sail ripped free from his grip and Mecho's entire body hung straight out and vibrated in the wind like a blown out sail. Nassor could not believe that any man could hang on under such force and expected to see his good friend fall to his death at any moment.

While the three stared in horror at the plight of their friend, the sail was torn from their grip, and with a report like a violent thunder clap it filled and strained against the sheets that were tied off below. In that moment all attention was called back to the task at hand and Mecho was momentarily forgotten.

Suddenly, in the dim light of dusk, through the storm they recognized the treacherous sands of Syrtis dead ahead. The dreaded quicksand trap on the shore of Claudia Island had ensnared many a ship and was now in position to claim Shanesse. Even though they were aware of the imminent danger ahead of them, the ferociousness of the storm and intensity of the workload had diverted their attention from the fast approaching shoreline. With the small storm sail set, Shanesse seemed to leap forward as the two helmsmen strained on the wheel to bring her about. Now as they steered away from the danger, fear flooded their thoughts for an instant as they realized how narrowly they had escaped losing both the ship and their lives.

But had they indeed lost a life? With heart stopping panic Nassor remembered Mecho, and with dread turned his eyes, glancing to port expecting the worst. He was astounded! Somehow, by a miracle of the gods, Mecho had survived his body being whipped around by the wind and the violent movement of the ship, and was climbing down with Ulray. Shaking with relief, Nassor focused on his own grip, as he descended to the deck. The gods had been watching after all! How could he ever have doubted them, he thought with both guilt and relief coursing through his veins.

As Shanesse's course took them away from the deadly quicksand region of Syrtis, Nassor found little comfort knowing that they were sailing directly back into the violent seas that they had briefly taken refuge from. He realized they had done all they could for Shanesse, and being completely exhausted, Capt. Warnken's orders for him to go below were a great relief. Even with the very genuine possibility of being thrown out of his bunk onto the floor by the erratic oscillations of the ship, Nassor found the conditions below preferable to the option of being washed overboard while working topside. On deck, the violent wind and churning water was so bitterly cold that, even in the dark, with the vile stench and stomach turning sounds of retching, the little bit of warmth Nassor found sleeping in his wet gear seemed like a luxury. As he climbed into his pitching and rolling berth, Nassor's thoughts traveled deep into the belly of the ship. He did not envy the sailors at all who were chosen to man the pumps, but theirs was a very important job, as they struggled relentlessly to keep the precious cargo dry and Shanesse afloat. Nassor along with every member of this dedicated crew made it their highest priority to protect the cargo and the passengers without concern for their own wellbeing.

The passengers too had been mercilessly battered in their quarters, and Nassor's concern for them was great. The sailors looked forward to going below because of the intensity topside, but the unfortunate passengers were becoming increasingly distressed as they tried to maintain some semblance of sanity while confined below deck. Seasickness was more prevalent among the passengers due to their lack of experience at sea. Most of them had not yet recovered from the long days of struggle to make Fair Havens. Yet not one of them considered that part of the journey at all difficult compared to the previous twenty four hours. Not understanding the full import of the situation, their relief was short lived as Shanesse sailed in behind Claudia Island. "Finally," they rejoiced, "the storm has subsided. We are safe at last!" Premature in that emotion, their hopes were once again dashed as the ship left the protection of the island.

Almost immediately they found themselves back in violent seas and within the hour, the storm sail blew out. Nassor heard it go with a mighty crack followed by a high pitched vibration in the rigging. The whole ship shuddered as the sail disintegrated, disappearing into the night. The passengers were once again fearful for their lives, thinking that Shanesse was beginning to break up.

Overwhelmingly discouraged and afraid, they wondered how long they could survive in a storm so severe. Ignorantly discussing among themselves their plight and perhaps imminent demise, fear grew and threatened to consume them.

How foolish is that? Nassor mused. That kind of talk will only produce more chaos and uncontrollable terror. I pray to Poseidon, god of the sea, to save us from this storm, and that we won't be forced to constrain panic-stricken passengers.

Although the passengers had no obligation in protecting the ship, they could not drop their guard for a moment, for if they were not vigilant, holding firmly to something solid, they would be thrown about their quarters, with collision and harm unavoidable. During daylight hours there was minimal light below deck, but at night the darkness was nearly impenetrable, making the most agile person an easy target for injury. Several of the less careful passengers were showing a number of severe bruises, and attitudes were rapidly degenerating. Julius, the centurion, and his detachment of soldiers with their prisoners appeared to be doing much better than most of the other passengers. Being in excellent physical condition and mentally disciplined, Julius garnered a great deal of respect from Nassor. What little order there was in the passenger quarters seemed to be coming from his area.

Trying to get some rest while being tossed about in his bunk, Nassor contemplated the situation at hand. If you combine two hundred strangers filled with raw fear, many bruises and the news that you will have to winter in a foreign city; mix in a lot of grumbling and complaining and then agitate continuously for twenty four hours, you certainly have an extremely volatile situation on your hands! As long as this storm persists, there isn't much anyone can do to improve the situation. As for that Paul fellow, he thought, there is an unusual calm that he has exuded throughout this terrifying ordeal. There is something eerily weird about that man, and I don't like him. Why did he have to voice his opinion about this trip? What does he know anyway? He's not even a sailor! Somehow though, I can't erase his words from my memory, and with all I'm responsible for in the frenzy of this storm, I DON'T NEED THAT RIGHT NOW! ☞

Chapter 2

Apphia's Apprehension

༄

That evening as she quietly prepared food for the family, Apphia felt a bit discouraged. She sensed the baby kick in her womb and looked over to the small shrine and altar in the corner, and prayed it would be a boy. She had slighted her husband Beryl by having four girls and only one son. She prayed to their household gods, 'lares', regularly for favor; her greatest desire was to have another son for Beryl. Apphia knew that sons were of great value, not only carrying the family lineage but also working as apprentices with their father. Beryl was a master craftsman, building couches, wooden chairs and tables in his shop by the house.

Their sons would learn the trade working with Beryl just as he learned from his father. People came from far and wide to buy Beryl's furniture. Apphia understood, having sons to raise up in the family business would help them all. She really appreciated Beryl; he worked long hours and saved as much money as he could. He was a good man! But one thing Apphia was keenly aware of was Beryl's deep concern, in fact his great apprehension, no, it had become his very deep seated anxiety, regarding their eldest daughter getting married. One may think that was a bit of an overreaction to a daughter getting married, but this was Rome. A dowry must be paid to the bridegroom and his family on the day they wed. The dowry was a substantial amount of money or property, equivalent to what it would cost to support their daughter for the rest of her life. Beryl felt the pressure! But the bigger problem remained, they had three more daughters and for that Apphia blamed herself.

Odilia our oldest is fifteen now and quite grown up, Apphia pondered. She will make a good wife. She's healthy, and I'm sure she'll be able to have children. Glancing in the direction of the family 'lares' Apphia corrected her thoughts and said aloud, "I'm sure she will be able to have sons." Roman culture dictated that a wife who could not bear children would be divorced because her husband needed sons to carry on his family name.

Being young, infertile and without a husband, a woman may as well be dead. She had no family to return to, having terribly disgraced her father by getting divorced after he paid the dowry for her marriage. If she was beautiful she could briefly support herself by frequenting the evening dinner parties at the baths but that was completely demoralizing, and short-lived. Often divorced women would sell themselves as slaves, working as forced labor for the remainder of their lives. Some extraordinarily agile and physically fit women would sell themselves to the lanista as gladiators. They were branded and pledged an allegiance to their lanista to the death. The lanistas were low on the social scale, making a profit by training, selling and renting gladiators. Living conditions of a gladiator were harsh as their company consisted of captured fugitives, criminals and prisoners of war. But as profitable investments, gladiators received better food, housing and medical attention than the average Roman.

Apphia being a feisty young lady had often reasoned that the life of a gladiator was an attractive alternative for these women, because although they trained vigorously and faced death two or three times a year in their competitions, the possibility remained of becoming famous. As a renowned hero of the games, they were paid well enough to buy their freedom and live the rest of their lives on the proceeds. The remarkable thing about a woman who achieved this status was not only that she redeemed herself socially, but she was now highly esteemed above other women, being sought after by the upper class aristocrats. Men of great wealth with established families would relish the thought of marrying her. Even without a dowry! What a strange world we live in, she mused. If I worked that hard, for that many years and faced death that many times to redeem myself, I'd never be a feather in the hat of some aristocrat! I could live a pleasant life anywhere I please. What am I thinking? Beryl is a good husband and father. He always recognized our children when they were born. We live in a nice home, and we enjoy good food. The closest I've come to facing death is in childbirth, and even in that the first one is the most difficult.

Apphia continued reflecting on life. Beryl waited until Odilia was fifteen to allow the arranged marriage. I think he saw how difficult it was for me when we got married. I was thirteen and he was twenty four when our marriage was arranged. I would never complain, and Beryl knows that but at thirteen taking care of the house, cooking the meals, working outside the home to earn extra money and being pregnant with Odilia was tough. I think that's why he recognized her. I know he was terribly disappointed when his first child was a girl, and I was scared. But when the midwife laid her at his feet he picked her up, smiled and held her close. I know the responsibility rests squarely on his shoulders. It's his decision, but I was so scared. How could I bear seeing my beautiful baby girl be exposed? I knew all too well that if he wouldn't recognize her, I would be required to leave her to starve or die from exposure. No wonder the babies that aren't recognized are often given to the river. But Beryl picked her up and smiled. Only then did I start breathing again. I have a good husband; I am so fortunate. Thank you god, Apphia thought, but please have this baby in my womb be a boy.

Apphia spent the morning in the fields with their two oldest daughters, Odilia and Francis. It was harvest time, and they could earn a little extra money working on the neighboring farm. But tomorrow she would accompany her good husband to the village north of them. Beryl would be delivering a table with six couches to a customer, and Apphia's goal was to visit the linen shop. Actually he liked when she chose the fabric for the couches because she was better with colors than he. But that was not important, they liked spending the day together. He could use her help unloading the table and couches, too. This table was moderately heavy. It had three sides each of which was large enough to fit two couches. Beryl made it in sections and fastened them together after they moved it into their customer's dining room. It set low to the floor to fit the couches. The more influential folks always reclined at the table. The couches were wonderful for dinner. A guest could slip off his sandals, the servant washed his feet, and he comfortably reclined on his side at the table. The table had three sides so after dinner you could just lay back and enjoy the evening entertainment with no one obstructing your view. All the locals agreed that Beryl's couches were of the most comfortable that one could buy, and Apphia did her best to choose the perfect fabric colors to compliment their rooms. The master craftsman and his wife found it completely satisfying to see the smiles of appreciation when their customers first laid eyes on their new table and couches. Beryl frequently made many of the regular taller type tables which were used mainly in the kitchen area where the ladies stood to prepare food. The commoners also used the same taller tables with chairs in the dining area because they were less expensive. Those who can afford it much preferred reclining at the table. Beryl favored building the finer furniture and had become well known for his excellent craftsmanship. Increasingly, most of his work involved building the low reclining type tables with couches. The work was more intricate and elaborate but he gained a great deal more satisfaction out of these jobs and also earned considerably more money.

Preparing for the evening meal, Apphia baked wheat bread and Odilia prepared some herbs and spices with the mortar and pestle. She was making garum, a delectable sauce enjoyed throughout Rome, used to enhance many meals. Apphia thought, what a pleasant girl. I'll miss her when she gets married next month.

"Mom," Odilia asked, "How do I do this again?"

"Have you prepared all the herbs?"

"I think so," she said with that serious concentrating look. "I have the oregano, celery, fennel and dill all mixed together. Now I just spread it on the bottom of this container, right?"

"Don't forget the coriander and the mint," Apphia said, giving her a reassuring glance. Apphia stepped in and helped a little too much over the past few years, but sometimes it just seemed easier to do it herself than showing the girls how to do things over and over. Now Odilia was feeling the pressure, she would be expected to prepare these things for her family soon, and mother would not be looking over her shoulder to make sure that it was done right.

"Sometimes I think you're trying too hard Odilia. Don't worry about it; you'll do fine," Apphia said reassuring her. "You're right; put a layer of the herbs on the bottom," she said holding up the container. Then motioning with her hand, she pointed to the different levels as she explained. "Cover them with a layer of small fish. If the fish are too big, just cut them in pieces. Cover the fish with a layer of salt about two fingers deep then start your next layer of herbs, filling your container to the top with the layers." Smiling at her, Apphia set the container on the table and thought back to how bad her cooking was when she just got married, but now wasn't the time to tell Odilia that.

"How long do I let it in the sun before I mix it?" she asked.

"Leave it about seven days before you mix it the first time. Then mix it everyday for about twenty days, and it'll turn to liquid. After that it's ready my girl; that's all that's to it," she said giving her a wink and a smile.

"But yours is the best, Mom. Remember when we visited Veturia. Her garum was so bad," she said making a face and shaking her whole body like she could taste it right now.

Memories of Veturia rolled across Apphia's mind like the dark clouds of a storm. Beryl could always tell what Apphia was thinking and now Odilia was picking up on it also.

"Sorry, Mom," Odilia whispered, "I didn't want to make you feel badly, I wish she wouldn't have died." Then standing up and looking at her mom with that sparkle in her eye reflecting her young and innocent love for life she said, "I liked going over to visit. Her children were fun, we always went down by the stream and caught frogs. Her husband must have been very pleased with her, three boys!"

Apphia quickly looked away as her face clearly reflected some dark and painful details that had unexpectedly surfaced.

"What's the matter Mom?" Odilia asked with a surprised look.

Swallowing a huge lump that had suddenly obstructed her throat with a tear trickling down her cheek, Apphia explained. "Veturia had six children, three were girls."

"What do you mean, Mom? I never knew that," Odilia exclaimed with even more of a surprised look as her jaw dropped and her eyes opened wide. Gathering her thoughts, Odilia said, "No Mom, Veturia died young. She was only twenty seven years old." Then with a puzzled look she asked, "Wasn't she?"

"Yes," Apphia answered softly. "She was only twenty seven years old, but she was married at eleven and her first child, a girl, wasn't recognized by her husband."

With tears welling up in her eyes, Odilia understood. Looking around to see that they were still alone she quietly asked, "How could someone let her baby die?"

Looking her straight in the eye Apphia said firmly but quietly, "It's not your decision Odilia, it's a decision for your husband, and he doesn't owe you an explanation. Don't forget that!"

"But three girls?"

"Yes, you know there's five years between the oldest boy and his younger brother. Two girls were exposed before the next son was born."

Odilia worked very quietly as they prepared the remainder of the meal. Then she spoke softly and quietly, "Daddy is really a wonderful husband isn't he? I hope my husband is just like him!"

Chapter 3

The Cargo Crisis

The night had been long, cold and difficult, and with the dawn of the second day Captain Warnken called his crew together. His face in the dim morning light told the story. Captain, a very solid man who rarely expressed emotion of any kind, simply faced challenges as they arose. The continued intensity of this storm was beginning to wear on even this experienced seaman, but as usual he would not let his men see his strain. His jaw was set and with eyes that appeared to stare right through the crew he spoke with firm resolve.

"Shanesse will not stand up to another day of this brutal abuse. We have no choice but to drastically lighten the ship if she is to be saved. The men on the pumps are already having a very difficult time keeping up with the seawater that's coming through the planking and our structural timbers are being overstressed to breaking point. If even one of them lets go, we will break up and go down. We have two hundred and seventy six lives aboard, and I have made my decision. The cargo has to go today or we shall all die. I don't have to tell you how difficult it's going to be. We can't simply open the cargo hatches; that would be immediate disaster with our decks awash as they are. You all know what to do men."

With a very uncompromising look at his crew the captain continued, "Be on the alert when you take the lashings off the containers, especially when you have to break open the larger ones to work the contents up through the gangways. I don't want you dead!" He said forcefully. "We are doing this to save lives, not lose them. If you get careless," and he paused, now looking at them as respected friends, not just as his crew. "If you get careless, some of you will die today…" Now looking down at the floor, speaking quietly just so they could hear his voice he added, "…and that simply is not acceptable."

What a leader! As rigid as Captain Warnken could be at times, and as resolute in his decisions, he was just as determined that there be no loss of life, even though each one of them had no doubt that there would be hell to pay when they arrived without their cargo. Small wonder that the crew would be willing to stand with him without question in the trial that was sure to come. There will undoubtedly be the loss of their precious cargo carrier Gold Seal of Caesar, but that seemed a small price to pay in return for their lives.

Captain Warnken hesitated and then continued, "I will speak with our passengers and explain the need to lighten the ship. At this point I am certain we will have their full cooperation. The only personal items to remain aboard are the clothing you're wearing and if we don't get this done quickly you won't need those either. Ulray bring twenty men, we'll go forward to the passenger quarters. Nassor, you're in charge of the cargo, so take every man who isn't working topside or on the pumps below. Carry on then, and may the gods be with us all!"

Nassor knew the cargo detail was no easy task. But regardless of the difficulty, they would lighten the ship and lose no one in the process. He formed a line of men from each of the cargo holds to the nearest gangway to the deck and would rotate the few men who had to work topside in the wash area with those below. Mecho helped him position each man in the line as well as possible, so that they could brace themselves against the rolling and pitching of the ship and pass the cargo from hand to hand. With strict instructions for the men in the holds, Nassor shouted over the ominous groaning and creaking of the ship,

"Keep your knives sheathed at all times unless you're actually cutting the lashings free. One at a time! One at a time! Only release one container at a time and be sure you have plenty of help keeping it under control as you break it open to pass the contents topside. Move as quickly as possible but do not release more than one container at a time. If you can open it without releasing its lashing lines that will be the best."

Each crew in each cargo hold had been given some tools to pry open the larger wooden containers. They began the hazardous work below, and Nassor worked his way up to the deck with the first pieces of cargo. As he forced open the small hatch at the top of the stairway he was instantly reminded of their perilous situation. Cold water came rushing down over him as he was assaulted by the torrential horizontal rain. The deafening scream of the wind in the rigging sent fear coursing through his straining muscles. This was going to be another dreadfully grueling day!

It was nearly noon as close as anyone could tell and still no sun had been seen. The work was exhausting and the weary battered men struggled with pieces of cargo both large and small. The stairway was never meant for loading and unloading cargo, and this would have been a difficult task even with Shanesse quietly at the dock. The most difficult thing Nassor was contending with by then was timing the transfer of cargo to the open deck between the large looming waves. The sailors out in the horrendous weather had to get their cargo over the side without being crushed or washed into the sea by the wall of water crashing on deck. Each man was secured by a line that was lashed to the mast. The tether line was only long enough to allow them to get to the rail, but would not allow them to be washed overboard as they hurled the pieces of cargo into the sea. It was an extraordinarily dangerous job, but despite the challenging circumstances the men fought the storm with uncommon bravery. Everyone knew that their lives depended on defeating this relentless adversary.

Some of the crew had just returned from the forward passenger quarters where conditions had deteriorated at an alarming rate. The seasickness medication flowed freely but had little effect. A majority of the two hundred persons aboard suffered from severe motion sickness and had expelled their stomach contents. Those who did not mind the motion initially had succumbed to the dreadful stench of the vomit that was awash on the floors. Working in that area had become treacherous as everything was extremely slippery and slimy. Captain Warnken helped bind the wounds of multiple passengers who had received cuts and gashes from being flung about their nauseating quarters by the pitching and rolling of the struggling ship. One of the crew, having taken a serious fall down the entryway stairs while carrying a large travel chest, was having trouble breathing, apparently having fractured a few ribs when it fell on top of him. Another suffered a bloody gash on the head as the two had collided in the mishap.

After completing their job forward, Captain Warnken had ordered an hour of rest as the men were on the verge of collapsing from exhaustion. He noted that the amount of personal gear was plainly astounding. Knowing that it was customary for travelers to literally take most of their belongings with them, he had figured it should have taken an hour or so to throw it over the side. But nearly five hours later they had finally completed the job. He allowed the detachment of soldiers to keep one weapon each and their paperwork but other than that, everything went. Most of the passengers were more than willing to give up their possessions in return for their lives; others were weak and listless simply trying to survive for a few more hours. Amazingly enough a few very distressed people, clinging to the familiarity of their belongings, would not give them up on their own. Other passengers, considering the preservation of life more important, helped the situation by relieving them of their goods and giving it to the sailors to throw overboard.

After what seemed like only five minutes, although an hour had passed, Captain Warnken stood up and commanded everyone's attention. He shared the somewhat encouraging news. "The pumps are keeping up, even with the personnel hatches having been open for most of the day. However, the fight is not yet over. Shanesse is significantly lighter already, but it is not enough. We must remove the remaining cargo without delay! This storm is still destroying her as she is too heavy for the tremendous wave action we are experiencing."

Each man took his place mechanically and with little complaint, even though some were vomiting again from overexertion. The unloading process continued for another four hours. Shanesse began rolling notably more and rising and falling sharper as she rode higher in the water. It was of course, less stressful on her, but the job of removing the cargo had become increasingly difficult as the sailors battled intense fatigue as the ship rolled with increasing fervor.

Nassor set about helping Mecho with some exceptionally heavy wooden boxes. They opened one of the containers labeled tools and found eight smaller packages inside. The first piece Nassor took from the top was outstanding. Even with the extreme fatigue associated with the day's project, this incredibly detailed wooden block caught his eye. It had intricate carvings and very unusual grain patterns and was inlaid with ivory designs, accented with precious stones in gold settings. He had an eye for fine craftsmanship and what an extraordinary masterpiece he beheld. As he handled it, the whole top lifted to one side on hidden hinges. Inside, perfectly fitted and formed, nestled in a layer of fine cloth, was a set of the finest pieces of jewelry he had ever seen. Absolutely astounded, he admired it only for a moment when Shanesse rose to an incredible angle before plunging down the face of a rogue wave. At the same instant another wave caught the bow, and it felt as if they had run into a solid wall. Shanesse shuddered violently, and they heard the sound of breaking timber. Everything shifted forward, launching one of the sturdy wooden packages out of the box labeled "tools," smashing Mecho's right hand against the super structure. Mecho cried out in pain as the package split open spilling gold coins all over the floor. The boxes containing gold were very heavy for their size and were labeled tools to mislead any inquisitive dock workers. Hearing the splintering sound struck fear in the hearts of the sailors. Three of them rushed to Nassor and Mecho's side to keep the boxes steady as Nassor helped Mecho up off the floor. In panic others began scooping up the gold coins and putting them in another box. Afraid for their lives they were shouting, "Hurry! Get this stuff overboard! We must lighten the ship!"

Concerned, Nassor examined Mecho's hand and was horrified to see the extent of the injury. The corner of the wooden box made a deep impression on the back of his hand exposing multiple crushed bones, leaving it in a very unnatural position. However, there was little they could do about it. Nassor helped Mecho to his quarters and wrapped his hand tightly with a strip of cloth then returned to his duties to save the ship and passengers.

Within another hour the sea had taken possession of the entire cache of cargo. They had completely unloaded the vessel, all one hundred and seventy-five tons of cargo, up the stairs and through the personnel hatches, an astounding feat in those conditions. Some sobbing, completely overcome by the exhaustion, others staggering like mere shells of the men they were at the start of the journey, the disheartened crew collapsed into their soggy berths to get some much needed rest, hoping that when they awoke the nightmare would have ended. The source of the splintering and breaking sounds that they had heard earlier had not been identified, and as they fell into their bunks everyone prayed openly to their gods that Shanesse would hold together for one more day. ⤶

Chapter 4

Linen and Love

⚐

Early the next morning, Beryl and Apphia loaded the new furniture on the wagon destined for the small but influential town north of them. Odilia remained at home watching the little ones. She cared exceptionally well for them. Apphia silently mused, it will be a big change for Odilia when she gets married; she is going to really miss her siblings. However, Apphia was delighted. Not many wives could spend the day with their husbands. Apphia sat close with Beryl in the cool morning air. What a pleasant day; the deep blue sky brightened as the sun prepared to climb into the eastern sky.

"What are you thinking about?" Apphia asked quietly as they had traveled for nearly an hour with no words, just enjoying the sunrise.

"Uh, yeah," Beryl said coming back from another world in his thoughts. Smiling at his wonderful wife he chuckled with that sparkle in his eye and said, "I was just thinking of how great it is, being able to spend the day with you," and gave her a little push with his shoulder.

Apphia laughed and pushed him back saying, "You were not," looking him right in the eye and giving him a big smile.

"Oh yes, yes that was what I was thinking about." He said with that sheepish grin he gives when he knows she has him figured out. "I was thinking of that spectacular breakfast we enjoyed together," and he paused, then added, "watching the sunrise through the trees, listening to the birds sing."

Apphia looked over at him with that simulated, puzzled look and said, "Oh, I must have been daydreaming. I never even noticed the servant girl come by with our breakfast. In fact," she said chuckling, not being able to hold that look of bewilderment, "I kind of remember chewing on some of yesterday's salt bread and eating an apple while I helped some guy load the wagon."

When they entered the village it was mid morning and the sun shone warmly as they passed the baths. The women were bathing and a few artists were there, sketching their masterpieces. Apphia thought, I'm not sure the men with the sketch pads are all artists, and from the look of some of their sketches, they surely are not masterpieces. Bathing times were much more a social activity than a simple scrubbing of oneself to get clean. The women went to the baths in the morning and the men in the afternoon, with the exception of these few male artists. Apphia thought with disapproval, they seem to be amusing themselves by hovering around studying the female attributes of this morning's bathers, attempting to disguise their motives with a sketch pad.

Apphia said quietly under her breath, "Can't you loosely packed individuals find employment?"

With a big smile of understanding and a slight shake of his head Beryl agreed, "my thoughts exactly."

They turned the corner and proceeded to their first stop of the day, the linen shop just down the street to select fabric for Beryl's next project. This shop marketed some of the finest fabric available for many miles around, and they had become good friends with Shendo the shop owner. Stopping the wagon in front of the shop, Beryl tied the horses as Apphia collected the pouch with the different color samples from their client's formal dining room. With eager anticipation, they both went inside.

Beryl and Apphia had much to be grateful for. They lived in a peaceful area with no worries about their things being stolen as they spent time in the linen shop. Shendo welcomed them with a smile.

"How's my favorite furniture builder today?" He asked as he vigorously shook Beryl's hand.

Beryl and Apphia slipped off their sandals, and he motioned for them to sit. His servant prepared to wash their feet.

Sitting down with them Shendo asked, "Have you had lunch?"

Beryl laughed and replied, "My friend, it's only mid morning and as a matter of a fact, we did have breakfast."

Apphia almost laughed as she thought back to the salt bread and apple they grabbed while loading the wagon early this morning. Another servant arrived with a plate of figs and nuts mixed with honey and a glass of milk for each of them. Shendo knew how to make his guests feel at home when they visited his shop. They relished the refreshments as they exchanged the latest news about each of their families and the local happenings. Then just as smooth as his linens,

Shendo led the conversation to the current task at hand, deciding on the perfect fabrics. Shendo was not only a good friend; he was a very good salesman.

Beryl complimented Shendo. "This customer came to me because of the exceptional fabric we used on his friend's couches; the colors accented his friend's dining room perfectly."

Shendo looked at Apphia and grinned, saying, "You know who we can credit for that!" Walking over and putting his hand on her shoulder he continued. "Apphia is one of the best color coordinators I know." Quickly he added, "And I know a lot of them." Pausing he thoughtfully continued, "If you didn't live so far away I'd have you helping me with some of my very discrete influential customers."

Apphia felt good receiving such a high compliment from someone like Shendo. He was no ordinary fellow. He and his family were highly respected and well known by many dignitaries.

In a short while they had made their selections and were saying their goodbyes. Shendo followed them out to the wagon chatting with Beryl as his servants loaded their purchases for them.

"You know Beryl, you make me look good using my fabrics on your furniture. One of my customers brought a couch into my shop that you made. They needed to match the fabric since their son had accidentally cut a long slash in it. That couch was very nicely built my friend. With craftsmanship like that I would be pleased to recommend you to some of my very discriminating customers."

Beryl turned and shook his hand. "Thank you, I would like that very much, and thank you for everything today. Once again it's been great visiting with you Shendo. You're a good friend."

It was mid afternoon until they had completed their delivery. Their customers were superbly dazzled with the new furniture and how well it accented their room, with many thank-yous, they slipped a sizeable tip into Beryl's hand as they shook hands on their departure. Now it was early evening as they hurried by Shendo's linen shop on their way home. Odilia would be anxiously awaiting their arrival as the younger ones sometimes did not listen to her as well as they should. It was only one day, and Apphia truly enjoyed spending time alone with Beryl, but she could hardly wait to see her children. Just ahead as they were leaving Shendo's village there seemed to be a great disturbance, possibly a riot. Expecting to see the soldiers ride in and break it up, Apphia was appalled at what they saw. It was a dinner party at the baths and she had never ever seen something that out of control. She had heard a bit about the dinner parties before but this? This! No, this shouldn't be. Traveling through the fray, making their way home, there were so many people completely inebriated with strong drink that Beryl had to lead the horses through the masses. Apphia walked alongside the wagon keeping the drunken guests from getting run over. Enormous tables were spread with a fantastic array of fine foods. Additional tables were covered with strong drinks of every kind. But the ground was littered with food; men and women were bathing together. Dinner guests, if one could call them that, were gorging themselves to the point that they could not eat anymore. Leaving the tables the guests would make their way through blankets that were randomly spread on the grass and disappear into a room around the back called the vomitorium where they would expel what they just consumed. Returning from the vomitorium they would either get caught up in one of the many orgies that were taking place on the blankets or simply return to consume as much food and strong drink as they could once more. This disgusting show of undisciplined behavior included the young and old alike, all being wealthier persons from the village and surrounding area. The irony of it all is that it was unlawful for women to have strong drink or even wine, punishable by death. Why? Because it was believed that a woman would be unfaithful to her husband if she drinks wine and an adulterous woman would also be punished by death. The women took their lives into their own hands joining these dinner parties, as it was normal practice for her husband, her father or any of her older male siblings to come and kiss her at various times to detect the presence of any strong drink. If she was disliked for any reason by her male counterparts, it may be her last party as strong drink and adultery abounded with all. Leaving that shameful fiasco was a relief as Apphia and Beryl could finally climb back on the wagon and continue their trip home, trying to leave that unpleasant experience behind them.

Beryl and Apphia talked of many things as they traveled home. What a satisfying day, with the exception of that foolish dinner party. Things were looking brighter for them financially; the tip Beryl received really gave his confidence a boost. The possibility of some furniture orders from dignitaries, or as Shendo said, 'some of his very discriminating customers' could increase their income substantially. Beryl confided that actually what he was thinking about when they left home this morning, was ways to increase their income. His concern was not only financial but the growing need for some assistance in his workshop.

Lightly patting Apphia's stomach, he confidently said, "This little fellow will help." As they drove the wagon up to their house, the children burst through the door with much excitement. They knew a trip to a neighboring village always included little gifts for them. With hugs, kisses and a bedtime snack of nuts and dried fruit, they waited for a goodnight from daddy. Beryl came in from taking care of the horses and putting the wagon away and enjoyed some dried fruit himself as the children excitedly told him all the events of their day with Odilia. ☞

Chapter 5

All Hope is Lost

ʦ

Daybreak of the third day and conditions had not improved. A weary and apprehensive Captain Warnken called the dejected crew together. They had fervently prayed that their gods would show them favor, but as they had struggled out of their berths they found no respite from the unrelenting storm.

"Is there any visible evidence of structural fractures?" he asked in a very troubled voice. Looking at each other, they silently shook their heads.

The crew had heard more breaking and splintering sounds during the night, but no one had seen any place in particular where Shanesse's structure appeared to be giving way. The captain seemed more unsettled that morning, and having made a desperate decision, he began bellowing orders once more.

"Nassor, Jag and Ulray, each of you bring four men, we are inspecting the ships structural beams now! I have to know what's breaking! Mecho, I do not want you killing yourself! Stay below! You cannot be working topside with your hand in that condition," he yelled, singling out Mecho who was looking pale and was clutching his injured hand to his chest.

Mecho's hand had swollen up to twice its size over night and was severely discolored. His face revealed the terrible pain he was experiencing but he would still try to do anything he could to save the ship. The sailor with the fractured ribs was also in excruciating pain. The roll of the ship gave him no rest as the bones ground together. Even he tried to get up and help but was ordered to stay in his berth. The crew was completely committed and now, following the captain's lead, had become desperate.

Captain Warnken continued, "Mecho, you oversee the work below and organize the men into seven groups. Get them to break up the furniture and throw it overboard. Anything that does not help hold this ship together must go! Throw the rigging overboard, the blocks and tackle overboard! All the tools overboard! Clean out the blacksmith shop, all the equipment goes overboard. The riggers room, clean it out, overboard! Mecho, save one storm sail and only enough tackle to raise it. Save the anchors and the skiff and save some food and fresh water barrels. Other than that, I am ordering everything overboard! Men, if you don't want to die today, I suggest you work with great speed and spare nothing. Listen to me!" He said, with a ferocious look of desperation. "Anything that does not help hold this ship together, goes into the sea, am I making myself clear? Now! Carry on with no delay!" he said, as he joined Nassor in search of the fractured structural beams.

As the crew absorbed the Captain's words, they knew this could be the end. He had ordered the very items overboard that controlled the ship. They would be at the mercy of the wind and waves now. The gravity of the situation propelled each one into action.

Benjobo, the ship's owner had endured remarkably well as the cargo was thrown into the sea the day before. He knew Captain Warnken and his crew would stand with him in trial for the loss of cargo, but he was notably distraught as they began breaking up his ship's furnishings and throwing rigging and sails into the churning sea. Without a word, and obviously afraid for his life, he began breaking up his own furnishings in the luxurious master stateroom, passing them out to the line of sailors reaching all the way to the aft deck. With the assistance of two sailors, he opened the lazaretto, a storage area below his quarters, and retrieved some exquisite items of great value. In wide eyed amazement at the sight of the treasures, the sailors helped him remove them without a word. Benjobo was a young, wealthy man of business who seldom showed emotion of any kind, and as he looked at his two assistants, whom he did not even know, with tears running down his face he asked the question.

"What good is wealth to a dead man? This was my life's savings with which I was preparing to retire in Rome."

Words of any kind were inadequate, so in silent sympathy they completed their project in the master stateroom. Benjobo's quarters were hauntingly empty; stark wood planking remained where plush rugs had once graced the room. The discriminating furnishings from master craftsmen around the world were gone. A hollow bang echoed across the empty room as the door slammed behind the men on their way to ravage another section of the stricken Shanesse. Taking his place in the line passing cookware, plates and other items from the galley, Benjobo silently and mechanically continued helping with the task of lightening the ship.

Removal of the heavy tools in the blacksmith's shop proved to be a great deal more challenging than first expected. The smithy's fire had long since been extinguished but the soft coal and the ash were collected in buckets. The bellows and all the associated pieces were being disassembled with much difficulty as Shanesse was now bobbing and rolling more sharply. The lighter she became, the more exaggerated the motion. Six fellows were working the anvil up the stairs with ropes, blocks and brute strength when it momentarily escaped their grip destroying a large section of the stairway. The mishap left this gangway virtually useless, but they somehow still reached the deck. Shanesse took over, rolling sharply to port and dipped her rail under the waves. The anvil tumbled out of control into the sea. They secured that hatch preventing more devastation by someone plummeting down the broken stairway, and moved to other hatches to continue plundering the ship.

Shanesse's great bounty of goods and wares, gold and stately furnishings, tools and rigging had all been offered to the sea. In return the sea released its clutches on the stricken vessel ever so slightly. Riding much higher, the deck had a great deal less seawater washing across it, which in turn relieved much of the strain on Shanesse. This had been the desired result that the exhausted crew was aiming for with all the extreme efforts taken to lighten the ship. It was a small comfort knowing that they had been successful. Now their new dilemma was the greatly increased and sharply amplified motion of the vessel. They had thought that it had been challenging to move around the ship during the first day of the storm, but the complexity increased many times over after they had disposed of the three hundred and fifty thousand pounds of cargo. On top of that, at Captain Warnken's command, the crew had tossed literally everything overboard that was not of vital importance in holding Shanesse together. They were now occupying the bare hollow shell of what was formerly an elegant, finely appointed vessel. Unloading that amount of cargo and equipment in a storm of this magnitude was utterly astounding, but the bedraggled crew had the bruises, injuries and aching muscles to confirm the great level of difficulty and strain.

The lightweight shell of the ship had become impossible to control with the confused seas and the unrelenting winds. The helm had been securely lashed off and everyone had been ordered below with only a single lookout stationed topside. A few men were on the pumps below and all others were now spending most of their time in their berths or wedged against something solid trying to endure one hour at a time. Captain Warnken returned from the forward quarters and quietly told Nassor that the passengers had lost all hope. It was deathly quiet up there with only the straining sounds of the ship and the muffled roar of wind and water. The screaming and cursing has completely subsided, even the crying and sobbing had gone quiet as there was little energy left to do anything but hold oneself still. The captain encouraged everyone to drink a little water as he noted that many were suffering from dehydration, but few even acknowledged his presence. Earlier he had ordered his crew to drink more water, and they had obeyed mostly out of obligation, but some of them, being severely exhausted, could not even make their way to the water. Nassor, Jag, and Ulray had been tending to the hurt sailors, as they now had twelve fellows bandaged up and out of commission from the day's battle with the storm. Nassor was concerned about Mecho, he had pushed a bit too hard that day with his crushed hand and had turned ashen. Jag sat quietly wondering if this was the end? He had proven himself as a sailor, one of the finest. But if

Shanesse went down tonight, his secret would go with him to a watery grave.

"Nassor," the captain said, looking at him and shaking his head in disbelief. "You and the men have done the impossible. Tomorrow will be better, get some sleep if you can."

Giving him a tired smile, and with great effort he stood up and made his way aft to his empty quarters.
⁊

Chapter 6

A Life in the Balance

❧

The wedding went very well; Odilia and her husband seemed happy. Odilia's absence was rather difficult for Apphia as her time for delivering the baby was near. Beryl was really feeling the pressure since a large portion of his savings vanished the same day 'his little girl' moved out. Paying the dowry for Odilia was not the problem; he loved her nearly as much as Burrus his only son. In fact what was bothering Beryl was the revelation that it took him fifteen years to save the money for one dowry. How could he afford to arrange a wedding for his second daughter in just three years?

This bit of reality weighed heavily on his mind for more than a few years. Most fathers did not have much time for their daughters, but Odilia was daddy's girl. If Apphia could not find her, she knew where to look. Odilia spent as many hours as she could with Beryl in the shop. Burrus, on one hand, at only five years of age had already started his schooling. Roman culture expected boys to obtain a working understanding of history, culture, business and government in order to one day become productive citizens of Rome. The girls on the other hand, spent very little time in school and learned most everything they needed to know working with their mothers. A daughter of a wealthy affluent family would at times have the opportunity to be educated, but they would not be considered citizens of Rome. The privilege of citizenship was reserved for men. Women had no rights in Rome, so having a fine husband with a skill, like Beryl, was a young lady's hope for a good life. Burrus would be in his mid twenties before his marriage was arranged. Much is expected of him as by twelve years of age he will formally become an apprentice in the shop with Beryl. So the difficulty remained, Beryl must wait another seven years for his apprentice and three of his four daughters will have marriages arranged and dowries paid by then.

Contractions had come and gone for the past several days, but this afternoon they grew much more intense and came closer together. Apphia sent Francis their second daughter to quickly find the midwife. Something seemed wrong. Beryl anxiously paced outside the door. I hope the midwife arrives soon, Apphia thought as she struggled to breathe. This baby is giving me a more difficult time than usual. Why the severe back pain? Laboring on the bed that she prepared earlier, Apphia positioned herself in the living area of the house so she could plainly see the shrine and altar with the lares in the corner. The last few months included fervent prayers each day; the gods must realize how important it is for this baby to be a son.

Another set of contractions came, "god help me," Apphia cried out. Gasping she wondered, how can this pain be so intense? I've had five other babies and I know they each were difficult, but I don't know if I can bear this.

Just then the midwife rushed in and reached out a reassuring hand. Apphia squeezed her hand so tightly that the midwife winced in pain and immediately knew something was wrong. When the contraction eased up a bit, she gave Apphia a spoonful of strong, fowl tasting liquid that made her mouth tingle and burned all the way down her throat. Having anointed the birth canal with olive oil to make things easier, the midwife now gently massaged Apphia's back and quietly told her she was doing great and everything would be alright. Apphia tiredly whispered, "The pain has been unbearable, I don't know if I can do it this time."

The midwife gently reassured her that she would be fine and told her to relax as much as possible between the contractions.

Two and one half hours of intense contractions and Apphia felt herself slipping away. She did not know if she was falling asleep or dying. Suddenly another strong contraction came, and she was instantly awake. She thought, I can't be dying; dying couldn't hurt this much!

The midwife excitedly encouraged her, "Push Apphia push, I can see baby's head!"

With renewed strength, Apphia pushed as hard as she could and prayed, god please...a boy. Resting and praying between contractions as well as she could, Apphia was greatly encouraged when the midwife said, "Baby's face up. That's why your back was hurting so much. Another good push is all we need."

And with that, baby was born. The midwife quietly laid baby at Beryl's feet as he entered the room. Intently looking at his new son, he suddenly realized that he had made the mistake that he solemnly promised himself he would not make. He looked at his baby's perfect little face and gazed into those beautiful eyes before he confirmed. No! No! It couldn't be. It was a little girl, and she reminded him so much of Odilia only fifteen years ago. His face turned white and it felt like his heart stopped. He could not breathe as a huge lump restricted his throat. His shoulders slumped forward and his knees became weak. Slowly backing away shaking his head, he silently left the room.

The midwife had been working with Apphia trying to keep her attention, standing in front of her not wanting her to see Beryl. Apphia's eyes widened in disbelief as she saw the most anguished look on Beryl's face that she'd ever seen. Suddenly realizing her baby was a girl, tears flowed as she struggled to keep from crying out. She desperately wanted to hold her baby as it too started to cry. A hopeless feeling flooded over her and she felt completely inadequate having had another girl. As Beryl left the room, she fully understood that their baby had not been recognized. Pleading quietly with the midwife she begged. "Can I hold her, please, can I just see her?"

The midwife said very firmly, "You must rest now Apphia."

Completely distraught, Apphia felt the room tilt and spin. Everything went black. ☞

Chapter 7

Two Weeks of Hell

꘏

Grueling hours turned into desperate days which in turn produced hopeless weeks as the unrelenting Nor'easter continued to batter Shanesse. Most of her feeble occupants had no hint of what day it was and even their trusted navigator was completely lost. He is a fine navigator, however no sun or stars had been visible for many days as they had been aimlessly driven about the Adriatic Sea. Or was it the Mediterranean? In that area two seas come together and no one really knew their exact location. Everyone aboard had completely lost all hope of surviving this storm over ten days ago. But today the prisoner Paul went about telling everyone he had a visit from an angel who was sent from the God he serves. Some of the sailors had visitations but their visitors certainly were not angels from God. At random times every day or so, someone would start screaming and cursing, apparently experiencing a visit from the spirits as no one could see what he was cursing at. Some would try and hide, curled up as tightly as they could in a corner, shaking uncontrollably with fear. Others would jump up and run violently straight into the side of the ship, being knocked unconscious by the impact. Not wanting to anger the spirits that tormented them, no one would assist the unconscious victim as his lifeless looking corpse slid back and forth on the floor with the wave action for the next hour or so. But now, Paul with more enthusiasm and vigor than had been seen from anyone for days, was saying an angel stood by his side and told him not to be frightened, that he would not die because he must stand before Caesar.

Nassor thought, that news in itself would have frightened any man aboard. What did he mean, don't be frightened, you won't die, you must stand before Caesar? There are no prisoners who wouldn't find standing before Caesar frightening!

The courage of this prisoner in his God actually brought a spark of hope to the distraught and dejected travelers.

"Listen to him," Nassor mocked, quoting Paul's words to anyone who would listen.

"You should have listened to me men…"

"Back in Crete you shouldn't have put to sea…"

"You brought this misery and loss to everyone…"

"We're going to lose the ship and be stranded on an island…"

"Now isn't that a first class 'I Told You So' if I've ever heard one?"

But the most amazing thing, Nassor mused, was that no one seemed to mind at all. If this God of Paul's could get them through this storm… and Nassor's mind began to wonder, who is this man Paul? I didn't like him from the very beginning. A confident prisoner? There's something strange about that in itself! But now, after two weeks of the most aggressive storm I've ever seen, he's… I don't know what he is? Listen to him. 'My God has given me all those who sail with me…' 'Because my God has given you to me, you won't die in this storm…' I know many a sailor who would strike him right in the mouth with words like that on any normal day. You don't tell a red blooded sailor that he has been given to someone! Those words may be acceptable for a slave, but not for a crew of first class seamen. But today, the only words that anyone seems to be hearing are those extremely confident words of, "No one will die…" "Not a hair on your head will be harmed…" "I have faith and complete confidence in my God…" "Take courage men, it will be exactly as was told me!"

Capt. Warnken apparently believed Paul, or at least had his confidence increased enough to bring some sort of order back to the ship. For many days they had not even maintained a watch. Everyone stayed below waiting to die. Now with a double watch in place topside, expectancy had begun to build among those below. At about midnight, on the fourteenth day, one of the sailors on watch burst into Capt. Warnken's quarters excitedly proclaiming, "Ulray believes we're nearing land."

Captain sprang into action, ordering ten men topside and placing an additional twenty on standby. Of course all who were physically able were now standing by, orders or no orders, the excitement level was on the rise. Ulray already topside grabbed the sounding lead. Jag burst on deck and rushed to his side to help check the depth. Twenty fathoms, Jag sent one of the deck hands to report to Capt.

Warnken but as he turned to go, Captain arrived by the rail.

"What do we have Ulray?"

"Twenty fathoms, Captain. I believe we're closing on that island Paul spoke of," Ulray said with much excitement, mixed with notable concern.

Every sailor aboard knew that the only thing worse than a storm at sea was running up on the rocks of an island in that same storm. Sending Jag and five sailors forward as lookouts, Captain ordered Ulray to take another sounding in twenty minutes. The visibility was still down near zero in the storm at night but experienced seamen could sense subtle changes in the wave action and hear the roar of surf in the distance if they neared land. It was more than a little job, retrieving the lead and rolling one hundred and twenty feet of line back on the reel with Shanesse bobbing like a cork. Everyone was quickly exhausted, the storm took more of a toll on them than anyone realized. The crew had exerted themselves far beyond the point that anyone thought was humanly achievable for the first three days, and this ruthless storm had awarded no rest for the weary since then. For eleven days they believed that at any moment they were all going to die and that in itself was extremely taxing on ones physical condition. Now, having endured fourteen days of intense physical abuse and having eaten no food, it unmistakably affected their ability to accomplish even simple tasks.

Captain Warnken spoke to Ulray "I too believe we're nearing land." Turning he said,

"Nassor take seven men and prepare the anchors and anchor lines on the stern. The last thing we need is to pile Shanesse up on the rocks tonight."

With that he disappeared below. Twenty minutes later Capt. Warnken was back by Ulray's side. "Drop the lead again," he commanded. Confirming their suspicion, the sounding lead bottomed at fifteen fathoms.

"We are nearing land!" Captain shouted. "Set the anchors off our stern."

Ulray came aft to help and they coordinated their drop so all four anchors bottomed as close to the same time as possible. They knew there would be an incredible strain on Shanesse and her anchor lines when they took hold. If they dropped them on mud the anchors would drag and they would continue running down on the shoreline somewhere ahead in the dark, but if they found coral or rock outcrops, they would promptly break their anchor lines and continue on to their demise. Specific bottom conditions were required for this maneuver to be effective. The anchors did take hold and Shanesse strained on the lines coming to a stop. Stabilized considerably, the decks actually became fairly manageable, which brought great relief as they nearly collapsed from acute fatigue. With tremendous strain on the anchor lines from the wind and the waves, Shanesse felt the pressure with her timbers creaking and groaning much like before they unloaded everything into the sea eleven days ago. Everyone aboard was praying to their gods for daylight.

Ulray and Jag came aft with Nassor. Watching the sea and the intense strain on the anchor lines, they decided that it would be a good idea to unlash the skiff and get it in place if they should need it. This could be a rough night Nassor thought. With much difficulty, ten sailors worked the skiff in position. Having only a few hours until daylight, the sailors anxiously waited. Intense fatigue and weakness clouded their judgment as the dominant question in each of their minds remained: Will we survive this storm?

One sailor blurted out the obvious, "The skiff holds twelve and there are ten of us. We have a much better chance of survival beaching the skiff than taking Shanesse ashore."

After two weeks of hell, mentally exhausted and physically spent, that made a lot of sense.

Jag instructed, "If anyone pokes his meddling head out the hatch, we're going to set an anchor off the bow, OK."

Nassor said, "We don't have another anchor."

Ulray spoke up, "They don't know that."

They began lowering the skiff. Suddenly two soldiers came topside. Weapons drawn they strode across the deck and with one swipe cut the skiff free. Falling into the sea, it promptly disappeared into the night.

"What are you doing?!" demanded Ulray.

Jag jumped right in there and shouted, "We were going to set an anchor off the bow; what do you know about sailing?" He continued, having become visibly distraught. "Do you want to die out here tonight? How are we supposed to set another anchor without the skiff?"

One soldier simply replied, "Paul said you sailors were abandoning ship and we couldn't let that happen if we want to live."

With no further words, they walked back and disappeared below.

"Paul said," Nassor shouted after them, "Paul said what... how...?" and words simply wouldn't come. This Paul is really beginning to irritate me!

Just before dawn, Paul asked that everyone meet together in the passengers' area. This man's tremendous confidence seemed to affect everyone. Having become rather pliable, no one questioned or argued with Paul's request. Captain Warnken agreed, so everyone was assembled. Paul stood up and said, "You have gone fourteen days without food, and you're going to need strength to get ashore. As I said, we will lose the ship but not a hair will fall from your head; we will all survive. Now I implore you, take some nourishment for yourselves; you will need it." With that, he looked at the cook and asked, "Could you find us some food, my friend?"

The cook disappeared below with two assistants. In a few minutes they returned, coughing, sneezing and gasping for breath. They had retrieved some sealed containers of salt bread but their eyes were watering, their noses were running and they could barely speak.

Finding his voice, the cook gasped, "The galley has been marinating in garum." Breathing the fresh air that was streaming through the open vents, he could talk better now. "A few large containers lay broken on the floor and I think the smell could exterminate a person."

Garum must have been awash in the galley for a full week, the air in that tightly closed room was simply overwhelming. This bread should be fine; it was sealed." Opening a container he handed it to Paul.

Nassor thought, if it wasn't for the hatches and vents being open in this area I'm sure no one could eat here either. The floors had been awash with vomit, human waste and blood for two weeks, diluted only by the occasional splash of sea water and rain coming through the hatches presently. He mused, the bilge area must be horrendous with all that filth making its way down to the pumps that they abandoned over ten days ago. Shanesse was riding high and took on very little water since everything was thrown into the sea. Taking some salt bread, Paul gave thanks to his God, broke it and ate it in front of everyone. Following his example, everyone ate some bread and all were encouraged greatly. With that, Captain Warnken ordered the ship be lightened by throwing all the remaining grain and water barrels into the sea.

"Leave the galley closed up, we don't need a thing in there anymore," he said.

Day had come. Going topside they could see a bay with a sandy beach but no one recognized the land. Capt. Warnken studied the waters and the beach for half an hour or more. Having organized his thoughts, he called Ulray and Nassor forward and gave them the bad news. With the small bay and the lay of the beach, it did not look possible to save Shanesse. The plan was to run her up on the sandy beach, giving everyone aboard the best opportunity of survival. The injured weighed heavily in his decision. Jag was helping Mecho out onto the deck; his hand was really looking bad. It went unsaid but no one would be surprised if he lost the whole arm by the time the doctors were through with him.

Shouting his orders Captain instructed, "Nassor, have the passengers remove all heavy and restricting clothing; I don't want them drowning in the surf on the beach. Jag and Ulray, get all hands on deck. Give them instructions on helping the passengers and those who are hurt get ashore. That surf will be pounding; it looks mean from here. Then prepare the storm sail." Mecho was adamant about assisting so Capt. Warnken said, "You will cut the anchor lines, Mecho. I will cut the lines lashing off the wheel and at the same time, Jag and

Ulray, I want that storm sail flying. We'll drive her right up on the beach. Nassor, have all the people amidships or aft, I want our bow running high to negotiate the surf. As soon as you have that staysail secure, I want all three of you back here on the wheel with me. This should be about as manageable as riding a humpback whale in a hurricane, and we have only one attempt to get it right. Report to me when you're ready and everyone's in position."

In minutes everyone was in position, Capt. Warnken turned and looked for Mecho who stood ready by the first anchor line. Hanging on with his good hand, with his knife in his teeth, Mecho gave Captain a nod and the order went out, "Cut her loose, Mecho!"

Bracing his back against the side of the ship Mecho took the knife in his left hand and cut the first anchor line. With a shrill whine and a slap, the line streaked through the air and splashed into the sea. Cutting the second one, he ran to the port side and cut number three. As soon as anchor line three streaked into the sea, the support beam and the deck boards holding line four fractured, taking a large chunk of broken and splintered wood including most of the stern railing with it into the sea. Mecho lay sprawled out on the deck, narrowly escaping the flying wreckage. Captain had already cut the lashings holding the wheel and the storm sail was being raised. Shanesse leaped forward as if she was anxious to end this journey. She literally surfed down the face of the waves then slid off the back as they passed by. Heavy following seas with a light weight shell of a ship, made tracking nearly impossible as the three struggled desperately with the wheel. Abruptly the sea changed. Entering an extremely agitated area, they discovered the waves were running in separate directions smashing together with incredible force. Still a considerable distance off shore they recognized, to their dismay, the devastating rough surf Capt. Warnken was concerned about was not only on the beach but they had sailed straight into a deadly trap. The foaming breaking waves were caused by two seas or currents coming together. When two currents come together, the waves are tremendously agitated even during fair weather. Colliding, the currents cancel each other's flow and drop any silt and sand they were carrying. The treacherous tumult of the waves is only part of the danger, as sand bars and shoals are ever-changing hazards in these places.

"Brace yourselves," Captain shouted. "It's going to be a wild ride!"

With three of them hanging onto the wheel, it was still proving to be very difficult to handle. Rising high on two opposing waves, Shanesse went roaring down the face.

"Don't let her broach!" Captain shouted, giving a mighty tug on the wheel. At that moment, Shanesse slammed into a sand bank, coming to an abrupt stop and the wheel spun violently out of control. The jolt knocked most everyone to the floor, many landing on top of each other and others crashed into the bulkheads and other obstructions in their path. A violent cracking sound came from deep within.

"Captain, I believe she's broken her back," Nassor said, "that sounded like more than just a bit of planking."

Capt. Warnken Bellowed, "Prepare To Abandon Ship!"

Gathering themselves together and realizing this was the end of the ride, the soldiers prepared to kill the prisoners, knowing this would be their destiny also if the prisoners escaped. Julius, wanting to save Paul, would not allow it. Shanesse began to break up as she was firmly aground forward; the waves began breaking pieces off her stern. A ship can take an incredible pounding as long as she is free to roll with the impact of the waves, but when she is hard aground, she is breaking up.

Paul spoke to Julius and Julius shouted the orders, "Anyone who can swim, jump overboard and swim for shore. Those of you who can't swim, take hold of a piece of the ship that's broken free and ride it ashore."

Nassor again questioning Paul's words was thinking, I've seen Paul pull off some crazy things on this trip, but if he thinks you can stand here in these pounding waves and simply climb on a piece of ship floating by because you need a ride to shore, that'll never happen! While swimming in the surf last year, we nearly lost one of our sailors as he was pummeled by a piece of driftwood that was in a wave half this size.

Most of the able bodied sailors were gone by now but Ulray, Jag and Nassor were helping the passengers time their jump overboard into the passing waves. If they jumped early or late, the trough of the wave affords only inches of water to cushion their fall onto the sand bar. Having understood in no uncertain terms the dangers of the surf while wearing heavy articles of clothing, the passengers were topside with light shirts or just undergarments. The wind and waves promptly stripped most of them bare, exposing tattered and bruised bodies that had endured two weeks of severe abuse.

Shouting at Jag Nassor said, "There's not much left that floats, wish we had a few of those barrels that we dumped overboard this morning. We could lash them together for Mecho and some of the other injured persons. We need -"

Stopping suddenly, not believing his eyes, a huge chunk of timber and planking from Shanesse' stern had broken free and lay quietly amidships as if someone was holding it steady. Two or three waves went by as at least ten people clamored and struggled to take hold of it. Then as if it was controlled by its own wagon master, it was caught up on the next wave and headed for shore. Looking to see if anyone else saw that, Nassor turned and noticed his three friends standing by the rail with their eyes protruding and their mouths open in complete disbelief. Another timber broken from Shanesse hull came alongside. People who were injured along with those who could not swim hugged it tightly; it too seemed to have a wagon master.

Mecho said, "Gentleman, I'll be taking one of those ashore."

They all agreed to accompany him and take the last of the injured with them. Floating toward the beach, Nassor again wondered, who is that Paul fellow? Is he a god, how does he know these things? And speaking of knowing things, what's he going to do to us for trying to abandon the ship this morning? I would sure appreciate if he didn't tell Capt. Warnken about that little exploit! ✆

Chapter 8

Shipwrecked and Snake Bitten

꒜

Shanesse, hard aground was being destroyed by the pounding waves and Benjobo could not bear to watch. He was one of the first to jump ship when he heard the orders; swimming for shore, he never looked back. Nassor had explained some basics of surviving large surf to one and all earlier this morning but everyone thought they were going to beach the ship. Now there is no leeward side of the ship to protect them from the brunt of the waves, everyone was on his own. The surf was brutal, slamming him into the sandy bottom he rolled and churned in the foaming water then as the wave rushed back to the sea, he found himself lying on the beach. Dragging himself away from the waves he collapsed by a small bush, slowly realizing that Paul's words were true, against all odds he was alive on an island.

Watching the pounding sea, Benjobo began to see others making their way up the beach. Amazed at their bruised and battered bodies, Benjobo felt sorry for them. Some were kissing the ground, others were searching for their travel companions and many simply collapsed on the sand. Debris from Shanesse began to wash up on shore. Every board and plank seemed to have a few people hanging on to it. In a short while, the beach was beleaguered with pieces of the ship, while a tremendous quantity of wreckage churned and crashed in the surf. Shaking his head in bewilderment, Benjobo was convinced that the gods were helping those unfortunate people get out of the water without being destroyed. Some natives of the island arrived on the beach and began helping survivors move further from the sea behind an outcrop that protected them from much of the wind. Others started a fire, and still others were arriving with blankets which they wrapped around the survivors who were now shivering violently. This was the first that Benjobo noticed, most of the storm victims had arrived with no clothing at all. As an islander gently wrapped him in a blanket he gradually realized, even though his clothing was of the highest quality money could buy, he too had only a few shreds remaining.

The storm subsided as quickly as it arose fourteen days ago. The wind slowed to a breeze but a cold rain persisted. Wearing little more than a borrowed blanket that these gracious islanders had given him, Nassor added his count to Jag and Ulray's numbers. Just as Paul had so confidently encouraged everyone on the ship, all two hundred and seventy six persons from Shanesse had survived. Astonishing, truly a miracle, Paul must be a god! From the able bodied swimmers to the seriously injured sailors, everyone had made it. The waves had thrashed them coming ashore, but who knows, maybe they had not lost a hair from their heads?

The islanders maintained an aggressive fire, trying to keep nearly three hundred people warm, on a cold day in the rain. It was a long narrow fire built in a huge arc to accommodate as many cold bodies as possible. Looking around, Nassor saw a long line of steaming blankets facing the fire on both sides. He barely noticed the cold rain as the steam bath created by his own wet blanket soothed his aching muscles. Nassor watched the gracious natives of this island, which they called Malta, quietly serving the people as best they could. Sipping on some sort of warm drink they gave him, Nassor was thinking, Paul knew there was going to be a storm and within hours of our departure we were overtaken by the worst Nor'easter I've ever seen. Now after the longest most excruciating fourteen days of my life, again within hours of our escaping the sea, the storm is gone. A most disturbing thought suddenly commanded his attention, it's not about the rest of us, the gods are trying to kill Paul! He came aboard as a prisoner, what terrible thing did he do? Looking around trying to see Paul, Nassor noticed that one of the islanders coming back with yet another bundle of sticks was wearing a blanket like they had given to all the shipwreck victims. Maintaining a fire of this magnitude was more than a small assignment. These Maltese folks are amazing! Here we are two hundred and seventy six helpless battered bruised and naked survivors without a single denarius to be found among us and they are taking care of us like we are friends. A group of them are putting more wood on a section of the fire right here by me and the one with the blanket is…

"That's Paul!" Nassor said aloud with an unbelieving type of question in his voice.

Standing close by, Jag looked up from his own little world of thought and asked, "What?"

Pointing at the only man in a blanket that was helping keep the fire going, Nassor quietly said, "That's Paul."

Jag whispered, "What's that man made of? Everyone else is so worn out that warming themselves by the fire is about all they can manage."

Nassor said, "I don't know what he's made of but the gods can't even kill him."

Jag looked at Nassor with a strange questioning expression but said no more as Paul had walked up and laid his bundle of sticks on the fire by Jag. Reaching out to warm his hands, a viper struck out of the new bundle of sticks, attaching itself to Paul's hand. Instantly recognizing the deadly viper, Jag shouted, "Naja haje!"

Jumping back, he knocked Nassor and three other people over as he found it simply impossible to keep both feet off the ground at the same time. Paul simply shook the viper off into the hot coals of the fire where it writhed briefly to its death. Gathering himself, Jag helped those who he had run over back to their feet. Excitedly Jag explained,

"I saw a Naja haje bite a snake handler who claimed to be a magic man on the docks back in Alexandria. His hand swelled up immediately and within the hour he was dead."

The Maltese folks told us they were sorry but there was nothing they could do to help. As whispers rippled through the group, all eyes were on Paul. Two men who were traveling with Paul, laid their hands on him and prayed to their God. The islanders apologized profusely having already really begun to like Paul who was notably different than the other shipwreck victims. Learning that he was actually a prisoner, they all moved away from him openly saying, "He must be a murderer, having escaped the sea the gods are still requiring justice." Julius came over to check on Paul, telling him how much he appreciated getting to know him and that he was so sorry it had to end like this.

Paul said, "I'm fine, don't concern yourself over this."

Julius sadly looked at him and asked, "How can you say don't concern yourself, your courage and insights saved us from the sea."

Paul reminded him, "The angel of the Lord told me I have to go to Rome and stand before Caesar."

Julius replied, "Yes, but what about the snake? You have just been bitten by a Naja haje, a viper, an asp, a member of the cobra family. Do you understand what I'm saying?" (As if Paul had somehow already forgotten or hadn't understood the severity of this snake bite.)

Paul stood up tall, looked Julius right in the eye and very plainly said, "Julius, the angel didn't mention anything about dying on the beach in Malta. This isn't Rome, and I haven't seen Caesar." Smiling, he turned and continued to warm himself at the fire.

Turning to Nassor, Julius said quietly, "The venom must have gone directly to his head; he's not making any sense at all," and quietly walked away.

The islanders did not understand what Paul was saying but they knew about the Naja haje and watched Paul intently expecting him to suddenly fall down dead. After watching him for some time, the whispers in the crowd changed. One said, "I believe he's a god." Another said, "He is a god; I heard him tell the centurion he talks to angels." Others said, "Look at his hand; it hasn't swelled up at all." "I heard the centurion say Paul saved them from the sea." "Yes, and their Captain said they lost no one in the shipwreck. Paul is a god!" The excitement grew until Paul heard what they were saying. He loudly and emphatically proclaimed the fact that there was only one true God, and he Paul, was simply a man who served the true God. The crowd quieted but many chose to believe their own versions of the day's events. Paul was a god. ☞

Chapter 9

Shendo's Prescription

⚑

Having struggled to load his wagon alone early that morning, Beryl could not keep from thinking about his trip up this same road only six weeks earlier. He and Apphia had such a pleasant day. She was simply wonderful to be with. What was he going to tell Shendo? How was he going to make the perfect color choices for his new customers? Walking into Shendo's linen shop, his smiling friend vigorously shook his hand telling him how glad he was to see him. Sitting down together, Shendo motioned for his servants to leave them.

When they were alone, he looked at Beryl with that concerned look of a good friend and asked, "My friend, what's troubling you? You look very tired and worn out. Is your lovely wife well? I see you're alone today."

Trying to change the subject, Beryl sat up straight, smiled real big and said, "Apphia is doing fine. The business is going well and I'm good. I just stopped in to choose fabric for my next project."

Shendo looked into Beryl's eyes and said. "Your face is smiling but your heart is sad. If you need someone to talk to, I have time to listen."

With that, Beryl pushed back the tears that were trying to overtake him and said quietly, "We had another baby girl, and I didn't recognize her. Apphia and I have only spoken a few words since, and I've gotten very little sleep."

"I'm very sorry to hear that," Shendo said looking down at the floor. "Is Apphia treating you well, or is she trying to make your life difficult? She should be extremely grateful," he said looking Beryl in the eye again. With a very serious gaze, he continued. "Beryl, I don't know of another family that has four girls. You have been more than generous, extending yourself well beyond what's expected of any of us."

Beryl broke in, defending Apphia. "She hasn't complained a word. She makes great meals, and she tries her best to be happy like she always was, when I'm around. I hate to admit this Shendo, but it's been me that I'm having trouble living with." Looking up and shaking his head he explained. "But I had no choice. I couldn't possibly raise another girl and pay another dowry. That just wouldn't work," and he slowly added, "I don't know how it's going to work now, with the three more dowries I have to pay."

After a full hour of pouring out his heart Beryl felt better. He had not been able to talk to anyone about it until today. As they sat for a moment, Beryl quietly said, "Shendo, I just can't get that little baby girl out of my mind. She cried for a couple of hours and I could hear her voice quivering as she shivered in the cold with her cry getting weaker and weaker. Then she just went off to sleep, but she wasn't sleeping, the midwife-." Beryl stopped short, tears streaming down his face. "Shendo" he said, "Every time I try to sleep, I hear my baby girl crying, 'Recognize me, daddy please recognize me'." Memories flooded in as Shendo recalled two of his own girls that he had not recognized. Glancing up, Beryl noticed Shendo too had tears streaming down his face.

Trying desperately to regain his composure, Shendo placed his hand on Beryl's shoulder and gently said, "You have to let it go my friend, you have to let it go."

Motioning to one of his servants, he quietly gave some instructions as Beryl sat with his head in his hands. After a few minutes Beryl took a deep breath and looking up he noticed a small drink setting in front of him.

Shendo explained, "This drink will help you get some much needed rest."

Beryl declined, pushing the drink back across the table to Shendo saying, "You've been more than generous with your time my friend. I do have to select some fabric and have a wagonload of new furniture waiting out front that I must deliver. In fact, your couch that you wanted for display is on the wagon also."

Shendo laughed and exclaimed, "Beryl, you look like we should carry you out to the wagon. Now listen closely because this is the plan. I will have your furniture delivered and set up by two of my best servants. They are familiar with working among distinguished clients and will represent you well. I myself will make your color selections, and you my friend will sleep soundly on the bed we have already prepared in the back room, not to be disturbed until it's time for your return home." With a broad smile he pushed the drink back across the table and asked, "Any questions?"

After six hours of the soundest sleep he had in over a month, Beryl awoke to an excellent dinner provided by Shendo. He could not seem to find words big enough to voice his appreciation for all that had been done for him today.

Laughing loudly Shendo declared, "You would have done no less for me Beryl. But I do have some good news, my servants have returned with a handsome tip for you from a very satisfied customer. Your customer had a relative visiting his home when the delivery was made. This relative was very impressed and ordered a matching set of furniture for his home."

Surprised, Beryl exclaimed, "That rest did me more good than I thought."

"Oh but that's not all," Shendo continued. "Three dignitaries from Rome stopped by today to pick up some very expensive linen that I had made specifically for them, and they saw your couch that is on display. Being openly impressed with your craftsmanship they ordered a huge table and reclining couches for twenty two guests. Knowing what you charge for the ones we delivered for you today, I simply tripled that figure for each couch and told them you would get back to them with a price for the table. They left a deposit of one hundred gold pieces, and asked that you would get started as soon as possible."

Having stopped eating, his jaw dropped open wide in complete amazement, "What did you put in my drink?" Beryl asked, "I'm having an interesting dream. I thought you just said you just took an order for me for just over twenty couches." Shendo nearly rolled off his couch laughing.

"**Just** now, you **just** thought, you **just** heard?" Laughing so hard he had tears in his eyes, Shendo tossed a sack of gold coins on the table and said. "You're not dreaming, you **just** have your words all mixed up. **Just** count that!"

Beryl offered to pay a large commission, wanting to make it well worth his time but Shendo assured him that buying the fabric for the project through his shop was payment enough.

Shendo then asked, "Seriously now my friend, do you remember me telling you a few times that your prices aren't high enough? You have a top quality product. You must add a little salesmanship to your craftsmanship. But now it's getting late Beryl, you should finish your dinner and be on your way. Sorex, one of the men who delivered your furniture today will drive you home. Give him a place to sleep overnight and he will ride the mule that we tied behind your wagon home tomorrow. I know Rome is a safe place to do business but you shouldn't travel alone with that much gold. I also know that Rome has some of the finest roads in the civilized world so you can stretch out in the back of your wagon on that fine fabric that we loaded for you and do a little more catching up on your sleep. You're looking much better, by the way."

Still trying to catch up with the furious pace of the fantastic things that were happening to him today, Beryl said very little as Shendo continued giving instructions.

"You should hire a first class craftsman to help you in the shop, there are a few out there that know how to build furniture better than sell it," he said giving Beryl a wink. "I believe this project for our dignitary friends in Rome will greatly increase your business. I'll advise you as much as you like, but it's your business and ultimately your decision." As Shendo accompanied Beryl to the wagon, he handed him a bottle of that strange liquid elixir that helped him sleep so well today and told him, "Don't drink this stuff every day, but it can help when you need it."

Climbing on the wagon, Beryl thanked Shendo again for being his friend and said he looked forward to returning the favor.

Shendo came close and said quietly "Beryl, go home and enjoy your girls. There's nothing wrong with that and take a little extra time with Apphia. She's a special lady, Beryl. She will be fine." Then very quietly he whispered, "You did what you had

to do, now just let it go. Everyone will be fine."
Walking away he turned and waved and in a
powerful thundering voice he said, "And that Burrus
is going to be a master craftsman just like his dad!
Have a good ride home my friend. See you in a few
weeks."

With Sorex on the reins, Beryl stretched out on
the fabric in the wagon. He looked up at the stars,
and tried to make sense of today's activities. Nearly
every day for four weeks, he had clenched his fists
and silently cursed the lares. The family gods, what
good are they? Where's my son? If it wasn't for
Apphia, I would have ground them to dust and
thrown them away, but I don't want to offend
Apphia. She prays to them every day. ☞

Chapter 10

Governor Meets God

W ord of the shipwreck had been sent to Publius, governor of Malta who lived extravagantly on a large estate near the shoals. Having endured the intense storm shore side, he was not at all surprised. Living by the shoals where two seas meet, shipwrecks were prevalent. The amazing thing about this shipwreck was that everyone survived, and there was talk of a god sailing with them. In times past, shipwrecks had been very profitable; many of the victims stayed in Malta as servants or slaves. But Publius reasoned with himself, shipwrecked on the shoals in a full blown Nor'easter, with nearly three hundred people and no casualties. Thinking aloud he said, "This truly is miraculous! One of the gods must be traveling with this group."

Publius contemplated the impact this would have. One of the gods walking and talking with us right here on Malta, surely things will never be the same again.

One of his servants arrived, and breathlessly he explained, "One of the gods is traveling with them!"

"Yes, so I've been told. Three hundred persons and no casualties, that is amazing."

Breaking in his servant blurted out, "Naja haje, Naja haje."

Startled, Publius launched out of his chair and shouted, "Where?"

"No, no, he's been bitten," the servant tried to explain.

Nervously looking around Publius asked, "Who's been bitten?"

"The god has been bitten," the servant continued.

Regaining his composure Publius plainly stated, "Then he's not a god at all, and he'll soon be dead."

"No, no, you don't understand; he's fine. The snake is dead."

By now feeling rather confused, Publius motioned to the chairs where he had been sitting and said, "Why don't we have a seat and go over this story in a bit more detail."

After a few minutes of explanation, Publius was getting very excited. Being eager to do all he could for this god who had come to their island, he summoned his servants.

Publius had directed his faithful staff and springing into action all were working enthusiastically preparing food, entertainment and accommodations for two hundred and seventy five people and one god. Four servants were headed into the village with horses, wagons and a long list for the marketplace prepared by the chef. They also had the job of choosing clothing of various sizes for the shipwrecked victims and a few extraordinary outfits suitable for a god. Publius himself joined the procession of wagons destined for the beach with his enclosed coach. They were going to transport the frazzled people through the wooded area back to his estate.

Arriving on the scene, Publius recognized the familiar sight that he had seen so many times before. Battered and bruised bodies wrapped only in blankets, huddled by a fire. Years earlier when Publius oversaw the beach rescue, he taught the locals to build the fire in an arc, having learned that the distressed survivors were comforted by being able to easily see each other as they warmed themselves. It was easy to locate the god as most of the people were keeping a close eye on him. Approaching Paul, he bowed deeply three times and welcomed him saying, "What an honor it is to have a god visit our island."

Paul quickly corrected him, emphatically repeating the fact that he was just a man who served the One True God. Publius of course agreed wholeheartedly, but knew that only a god could survive a Naja haje bite. Inviting Paul into his coach, Publius addressed the crowd and graciously explained that the wagons were there to carry them back to his estate where they would be his guests. He went on to explain, "There is a hot meal being prepared for you as I speak, and wagons will be returning from the village with warm clothing for all."

A feeble cheer went up from the crowd, as they were greatly encouraged and the injured were already being helped onto the wagons. Julius insisted on riding in the coach with them and looking at Paul for approval, Publius invited him in. Paul also invited two other men along with them, Luke and Aristarchus. Being that Paul was a god, Publius supposed a few personal attendants were to be expected, but then he would not know, never having a god ride with him in his coach before.

They spoke very little on the short ride to his estate as Publius was simply without words. What do you say to a god? Glancing at Paul's hand he could plainly see where the Naja haje bit him, but there was no sign of swelling. When they arrived, Publius showed Paul into a large hall where they enjoyed the warm drinks already setting out for their expected guests. Making sure Paul was comfortable, Publius quickly slipped away, instructing his staff to prepare a warm bath and went to his personal wardrobe to find Paul some of his finest clothing. Having collected one of his best, special occasion outfits, and something for Julius, Luke and Aristarchus, Paul's personal assistants, he returned. First escorting Paul and his assistants to his personal bathing area, he left them there with clothing and several attendants, then he came back and addressed the people.

"My wagons will return from the village soon with much clothing for you to choose from." Directing their attention to the far side of the hall he continued, "The bathing area is over there and the attendants are prepared to assist you with the things you need. If any of your friends were hurt, they are being cared for in the adjoining building to your right. Enjoy the warm drinks and make yourselves comfortable. In one half hour we will be serving a special meal that will be soothing to your stomach and renew your energy. Anytime you want to sleep, arrangements have been made in the other end of the building where they're caring for the injured. The storm is over, the shipwreck is behind you and you're safe. Please, you are my guests, I want you to relax and enjoy yourselves."

Evening had come and a few quiet conversations were going on here and there but most of the people slept soundly for the first time in two weeks. Publius had given Paul the finest guest suite on the estate with rooms nearby for Luke, Aristarchus and Julius and had not seen any of them since the meal. Publius and his staff had chatted with some of their guests and were amazed at the stories of their incredible journey. Many spoke of Paul. Some said he was a prisoner and Julius was not his assistant at all but a Roman centurion. Others insisted he was a god, speaking of his bravery and confidence on the ship. He foresaw future events including the storm, the shipwreck and everyone surviving. Paul even told them they would end up on an island and now, everything he had notified them of happened exactly as he said. Walking slowly by Paul's room, trying to make sense of all these varied and bizarre stories, Publius paused as he overheard Paul praying to a god who he addressed as his father. Excitement flooded his soul as he heard Paul thank his Father God for saving all the people on the ship, who apparently were given to Paul by his Father, for safe keeping sometime during the storm. Startled as he heard his name, Paul had just asked his Father to bless Publius and his staff for their kindness. Publius moved along as quickly and silently as he could, Paul probably knew he was outside his door too! Sorting through the facts Publius contemplated. Paul is the son of a god, he knows the future, these people were given to him for safe keeping, he lost no one in the shipwreck and the Naja haje bite had no effect on him. Arriving at the obvious conclusion, Publius now had no doubt. Paul was a god!

Three days after the wreck, things had improved to a great extent for most of the victims. Rest, good food and professional entertainment seemed to be working wonders. However some desires were indeed more than Publius could provide. For example, the local doctor had just informed Mecho that he could not save the hand. Nassor, Jag and Ulray seem to be doing fine but they felt Mecho's pain as he prepared to lose his hand and his position. Sailing was all he knew and he was one of the finest, but this loss would force him down to a second class deck hand. For Mecho that demotion would be far more difficult and painful than losing his hand. Likewise Benjobo had been listless and absorbed in distressing thoughts of the future, as were many of the passengers haunted by the disturbing questions. Would they ever be able to complete their trip or even be able to earn enough money to get off this island? What would they do when Publius' kind hospitality ran out?

Just after the noon meal, Paul stood up and addressed them all. Starting out he again emphasized, "I'm not a god, but I serve the One True God." With much detail he presented the good news of the Kingdom of his God. He spoke of Jesus, God the Father's only Son who paid the ultimate price for our redemption so we could become citizens of His Kingdom. Redemption at this point was a very interesting subject. Many of the people present had lost everything and wondered on a very personal level, who will my redeemer be? It was well known and understood that having lost everything your destiny usually included being sold as a slave. Your only hope was for someone to redeem you, pay the price, buy your freedom. Paul went on to quote the prophet Isaiah, saying Jesus had carried our sicknesses, weaknesses, and distresses and by the stripes that Jesus received, we are made whole.

Publius, intently listened to the words of this god, or Paul, or whoever this was, stood up and asked, "My father-in-law Gratus, is very sick in bed with dysentery, can these stripes of Jesus heal him?"

With no hesitation whatsoever Paul confidently replied, "Yes, God can heal him. Where is he?" This came as a great surprise to most everyone there.

"He lives right here on the estate with me" Publius said, pointing in the direction of a nice home a short distance away.

Nearly two hundred people accompanied Paul and Publius for the short walk across the grass to his father-in-law's house. Publius introduced Paul and stepped back as people crowded into and around the house, each trying to see what was going to happen. Paul prayed to his Father God and laid his hands on the sick man in the name of Jesus and immediately, he was healed.

This caused no little stir as the people were astonished when Gratus came out of the house, shouting and loudly praising the Jesus, in whose name he was healed. Leading the way back to the large hall where the remainder of the people lingered, Gratus exuberantly proclaimed over and over, "By the name of Paul's Jesus, I'm healed!"

Mecho had been quietly listening to Paul's words but had not accompanied the group, staying with the others who were injured as he was now running a high fever and his entire arm protested in terrible pain if he moved it. Hearing Gratus shouting over and over he is healed, clearly got Mecho's attention. A desperate hope came over him. Forcing himself off the mattress he was lying on, holding his hand high trying to avoid someone bumping it, he made his way through the crowd to Paul. Nassor saw Mecho, completely white wincing in intense pain, pushing his way through the crowd. Coming to his aid, Mecho collapsed in Nassor's arms. Fear jolted Nassor as he felt how hot Mecho was. He realized his friend had an exceptionally high fever. Trying to decide what to do with his friend hanging limp in his arms, Nassor wondered if Paul's Jesus could cure this high fever when suddenly he heard a booming voice over his shoulder as Capt. Warnken shouted, "Paul, over here!"

The crowd parted as Paul made his way to Mecho who was struggling to stand up. Holding out a severely swelled hand that had developed deep purple streaks running up his arm, fading in and out of consciousness from the intense pain, he weakly asked, "Can Jesus heal me?"

From behind, Nassor heard an earnest, "Please" quietly coming from Capt. Warnken.

Ever so gently Paul reached out and touched Mecho's hand and in a very commanding voice said, "Be made whole in Jesus name."

Mecho slumped in Nassor's arms and as everyone watched, the streaks in his arm went away and his fingers began to move. Regaining some strength, Nassor let go of him allowing him to stand on his own. Mecho knelt down on the floor with tears flowing and told Paul, "I believe your words about the One True God and His son Jesus, can I be a part of His Kingdom?"

A quiet, "Me too" came from his side as Nassor joined him on his knees.

"And I," Capt. Warnken said joining them.

After praying with them, Paul helped them to their feet.

Capt. Warnken said, "Thank You, Thank You, Thank You," reaching out his powerful arms, pulled Paul near and gave him a big hug.

A few feet away Ulray elbowed Jag who was standing beside him and said quietly,

"That sure softened up the Captain; I've never seen him hug anyone."

Jag, dealing with thoughts of his own did not respond.

Mecho felt like a full ton of weight lifted off his shoulders at that moment. For the first time he thought he could understand just a little, how Paul made it through the storm so well. With hands stretched toward the heavens Mecho proclaimed, "What an incredible God! What an incredible Kingdom!" Seeing his hand, and feeling no pain for the first time since it had been crushed, he moved his fingers and exclaimed, "Look at my hand, look at my hand!"

Spinning around he snatched Nassor's hand and with the commanding grip of an expert sailor shook it vigorously saying, "Welcome to the Kingdom my friend, welcome to the Kingdom!"

Mecho went about shaking hands with everyone saying, "Look at my hand, look at my hand."

Everyone in the hall was amazed beyond belief at the power of this One True God that Paul spoke of, confirming his words right in front of them with astounding signs and wonders. ⮞

Chapter 11

Elixir of Sleep

~

Apphia heard Beryl arrive very late in the night and the door close quietly as he came into the house. She knew how terribly offended he was with her for giving him another daughter. He had only spoken a few words since that dreadful day. She kept trying to forget the last pregnancy ever happened, and she had not prayed to those worthless gods in their annoying little shrine since. She had considered knocking one of the idols over while dusting that corner of the living room and accidentally destroying them one at a time. No one would notice, Beryl did not seem to pay much attention to them anyway. The gods apparently had no concern whatsoever for her and her family and in turn she had lost all respect for them. But Apphia was careful not to let her attitude show, as she had already terribly disappointed Beryl, and she was not convinced that life would ever be enjoyable again.

Beryl quietly walked into the room and stopped by the edge of the bed, leaning down he gently kissed Apphia. What! Her heart nearly stopped. Her mind was racing. What happened today she wondered? So badly wanting to ask him all about his day she thought it best to be very cautious, not wanting to destroy the first good thing that happened in a long time. Beryl left the room but returned in a few minutes and climbed into the bed. Snuggling right up close with Apphia he promptly fell asleep. Apphia lay there for hours, not able to sleep. She was sure something good had happened, but what? Beryl had treated her well these last few weeks but she knew that she had severely disappointed him and he said very few words since. Odilia had come to visit one evening after she heard the news, but it was not a good visit. She quietly told her mother she hoped to never get pregnant, and she refused to even look at her daddy. That was a crushing blow to Beryl. Odilia and he were always together when she lived at home. It was very difficult for him when she got married and left home, but that did not compare to the hurt on his face that radiated from deep within his heart when she avoided him on her last visit. Apphia had a thousand different thoughts racing through her mind. How were they going to pay the dowry for Francis? She was already twelve. What if Odilia has a little girl? Having my baby girl exposed was the most difficult thing that ever happened to me, but Odilia would literally be devastated. But worse, what if Odilia could not have children as she so foolishly hoped? After what seemed like hours, Apphia drifted off to sleep. She dreamt of a man who helped them to get things in perspective. She did not remember details, but she knew that somehow things had become clear and their lives had new meaning.

Waking early, Apphia found that Beryl was already gone. Hurrying out of bed, she dressed and came into the living room and was quite startled to find a strange man in their house. Returning from the kitchen, Beryl was carrying hot drinks for the three of them. Completely speechless, Apphia accepted her cup of tea and Beryl invited her to sit down with him and the stranger.

"No, no," she insisted, "I'll prepare breakfast for you two."

The stranger looked vaguely familiar but she sure could not place him. But what's going on with Beryl preparing the tea? Things are really getting chaotic around here she thought. Fear tried to step in, as the thought of being divorced for having too many girls crossed her mind. But she reasoned with herself, Beryl kissed me last night and snuggled close to sleep. That was not what you do when you intend to divorce someone. And the tea, what is going on with Beryl preparing the tea? Men do not prepare the tea! The most incredible thing was not that Beryl prepared the tea but that he prepared her tea also and offered it to her right in front of another man. In Roman culture, that is completely unheard of. A man would never serve a woman especially in the presence of another man.

Emotions struggled within her. She did not know whether to laugh or cry. She steeled herself to hurriedly prepare a first class breakfast. That skill was something she excelled at. Beryl often complimented her on what a great meal she could, as he said, 'pull out of the air'. Having the breakfast ready, she very forcefully told herself that there would be no questions. She would smile, make eye contact and serve the food. Inviting the men into the dining room, she smiled and served the food. Beryl told the stranger, "You see what I'm talking about, Apphia can simply pull a great breakfast right out of the air in no time at all." Looking at her he said, "Recline at the table with us my lady. I have some great news."

Apphia quickly set another place at the table and without a word, joined the men. Now things were really getting exciting, she could hardly contain herself. She quietly took one of the couches and did not say a word, but on the inside she was bubbling with excitement, wanting to dance and shout. Something good was happening!

Beryl looked at Apphia and smiled, "You're not doing very well," he said.

Almost exploding from all the pressure on the inside and wanting to lean over and poke him in the ribs Apphia, as calmly as possible said, "What?" She recognized that playful grin that Beryl would give her when he knew exactly what she was thinking because she could not hide it from him. But now she was trying her best to control herself, as she still had no idea who this stranger reclining at the table with them was. Beryl looked at her with that little sparkle in his eye that she had not seen for a long time and tossed an open sack on the table. Gold coins spilled out, and Apphia's mouth dropped open. Beryl was laughing now and Apphia could not take it anymore. She jumped up, went over to Beryl, gave him a huge hug and a kiss. Then suddenly remembering they were not alone at the table, she turned bright red and quickly returned to her couch trying to act as sophisticated as possible.

Feeling badly, watching Apphia trying so terribly hard to contain herself Sorex said, "Don't concern yourself with me, I'm Shendo's servant."

Beryl quickly interjected, "This is Sorex, he accompanied me home last night as Shendo didn't think I should travel alone with such a large sum of money."

Apphia smiled hugely, now recognizing Shendo's servant who she would have known immediately in Shendo's shop, but he took her by surprise in her own home. She looked at Beryl and said, "Would you like to explain what's-" Stopping short she turned to Sorex and said, "I'm sorry. It's nice to have you here Sorex, It really is. Thank you for accompanying Beryl home last night. I think we should enjoy our breakfast while it's warm, and I'm sure that Beryl can hardly wait to tell me where this came from," pointing to the bag of gold on the table and turning to look at Beryl.

Enjoying their breakfast, Beryl told Apphia all about Shendo insisting he get some much needed sleep and the whole story of the servants delivering his furniture, getting a great tip and another order for a matching set of furniture. He told of Shendo tripling his price and still getting the huge order from the Roman dignitaries that included the one hundred pieces of gold for the deposit. Beryl spoke very highly of their friend Shendo and all that he had done for him. Apphia thought of her dream and wondered if Shendo was the man. Beryl was so pleased to see the excitement in his wife; he had his Apphia back again. This was the lady that he loved. He was very careful to not say a word of his and Shendo's talk or of the wonderful elixir that helped him sleep so well. Finishing their breakfast, Beryl told Sorex to wait as he went out to his shop. Returning with an intricate carving of a horse and chariot, he carefully packaged it so it would not be damaged on the ride home. The carving had taken him many days to complete because it was highly detailed. Beryl only carved things for himself, as he really enjoyed it but was sure that he could never get enough money to cover the many hours it took to complete one. Trying to find a proper thank you gift for Shendo, he hoped the carving would help show his great appreciation. Thanking Sorex again for accompanying him home, Beryl and Apphia waved goodbye as he rode away.

Beryl hired an excellent craftsman that lived in the neighboring village. His new helper truly was a brilliant craftsman but lacked severely in people skills, which was the precise reason he could not survive selling his own furniture. Beryl left explicit instructions for Apphia, that when he was not around, no one was available to talk to the customers.

"Never allow the new man to chat with the customer," Beryl said. "He could destroy a business deal in five minutes."

Apphia and Beryl were pleased; it seemed that they had gained their life back. Neither of them ever discussed their baby girl that had been exposed, but time seemed to make things better. Within the year, Beryl's business had grown leaps and bounds. At Shendo's direction he had purchased a large building close by which greatly increased his working area and afforded more simultaneous production. It had a display room in the front and a sizeable working area in the back. Beryl's operation grew from the one helper that he hired immediately on Shendo's advice to a salesperson who worked directly with the customers in the showroom, three master craftsmen including himself and five young apprentice helpers working in his shop. Shendo had come out to his place numerous times and helped him with specific business details. As Shendo had said, the furniture for the Roman dignitaries suddenly brought tremendous demand as the upper class people greatly appreciated his precise workmanship. Workmanship was the focal point; no matter what the schedule and how many orders were waiting, the furniture had to pass Beryl's inspection before it went out the door. Beryl missed visiting with the customers as he also had two servants who delivered and set up the furniture for him, but business was great.

Some other things were not so great. Beryl continued to have difficulty sleeping, so he used Shendo's elixir of sleep, as he called it, regularly but it took more and more to be effective. Shendo had warned him not to use the sleep aid consistently. Having gone through the first bottle in a very short time Beryl asked Shendo for another. Shendo was concerned then already, and told him he should not use the elixir repeatedly, only to help him when it was really necessary. He had assured Shendo that things would get better and he would not need so much of it then. Finding a place in his own village where he could buy it, he did not mention it again to Shendo who thought he simply did not need it anymore. The elixir he was in search of contained an extract from the poisonous plant henbane which was used by doctors as a sedative. Beryl had started taking a stronger more potent mix of this sedative only to find that he had trouble remembering certain things. He had quietly kept his elixir of sleep unnoticed and had no plans of telling anyone about it.

Apphia came in one evening and asked, "Beryl what's bothering you?" She had noticed that he seemed to be fidgety and physically shaky. She suspected something was not right when he stopped carving.

Beryl loved to carve but recently he would begin to tremble and damage beyond repair something he had worked on for days. Beryl retrieved his bottle of elixir of sleep and openly explained to her,

"Shendo gave me some of this elixir of sleep a year ago and I used it frequently ever since. Shendo said to be very careful with it and not use it on a regular basis, only when I needed it. But I need it most every night and I still have bad dreams." Having said that, he laid down and fell asleep.

The next day, Apphia found herself alone in the display room with Beryl and quietly asked him, "Did you sleep well last night?"

He looked at her with a puzzled look and said, "Yes, ok I guess."

"No bad dreams?"

Startled he quickly looked away and asked, "What are you talking about?"

Apphia thought, he doesn't remember a thing about last night, and then it started making sense. He often didn't have a clue what she was talking about when she would mention something they talked about right before he went to bed. It must be the elixir of sleep making him forget.

"I merely wanted to know if you rested well?"

"Fine, fine, I slept just fine," he said and quickly made his way out to the shop.

Questioning herself, Apphia went into the house and making sure she was alone in their bedroom, she found the bottle of sleep elixir. No it's not me; he really is taking some sort of sleep elixir as he calls it, and it is hurting him. He always had hands as steady as a rock, now he gets the shakes and forgets things. Suddenly a thought flashed through her mind. That juice must also loosen his tongue. He spoke openly and plainly about the elixir, which he hid from everyone for a year, right after he took some last night. But now, he does not remember a thing.

Apphia did not want to abuse this newfound knowledge but she purposely came into the room shortly after she figured he had taken some of his tongue loosening juice. She asked, "How's the business going?"

Without hesitation Beryl said, "The furniture orders are pouring in, and it's hard to believe how well things are going."

This was very true. This last year Beryl had earned that much money that even after buying the big building, he had more than enough money saved to pay the dowry for his second daughter Francis. Continuing to test the waters a bit Apphia asked,

"Are you pleased that we already have enough money saved for Francis' dowry?"

"Yes," he said, "But it also makes me very sad."

Now he is not making sense Apphia thought. That elixir is making him crazy. "What do you mean, it makes you sad?"

Beryl dropped his head and quietly said, "I could have earned the money for another daughter's dowry. I didn't have to expose her." He began to weep softly as he continued. "I can hear her crying in my dreams, 'daddy recognize me, daddy please recognize me'."

Apphia began to weep also. "I'm so sorry Beryl, I'm so sorry," she said. "I prayed to the lares everyday that our baby would be a boy."

He straightened up with clenched fists and a fierce hatred in his eyes. "Those damned gods, I should grind them to powder. They have done us evil!"

Beryl's eyes were heavy from the medication, and he could hardly sit up. Apphia helped him lay down, and he was immediately asleep. She kissed him and held him tightly as she cried herself to sleep. Beryl is a good man, she thought. Beryl is a good man.

The following morning very early before the children got up, Apphia was making breakfast for Beryl, which she rarely did anymore since the business was going so very well. They had bought two slaves, one kept the house and the shop clean and the other did all the cooking which was quite a task as they provided lunch, the main meal of the day, for their employees also. But this morning Beryl was off to yet another meeting with some important individual in Rome who wanted a special set of furniture, so Apphia was serving him just like she used to. She was very careful with her words as she wondered if Beryl remembered anything of last night's conversation. He did not appear to remember but he seemed different today. He's probably no different at all, Apphia thought. I just know him better. He cared so much for our baby girl; it must have hurt him as much as it hurt me. Thinking about it Apphia was astounded. Beryl had never mentioned a word about their daughter before. The pain must be unbearable as he was apparently self-destructing on the inside. ↣

Chapter 12

New Life on Malta

꒥

Not only the injured survivors from Shanesse and those of Publius' staff that had suffered any illness were healed, but all those who suffered from sickness and disease on the entire island came to Paul and received health from the Jesus that he represented so well. The large hall on Publius' estate where they enjoyed their first meal was now filled to capacity each day. Mornings consisted of Paul teaching the good news of the Kingdom and a broad-spectrum of how this affected those who had chosen "The Way." Nearly thirty days had passed since Publius' father-in-law Gratus was healed and all who had survived the wreck of Shanesse enjoyed a very satisfying life. They were continually served and attended to in every way by the people of Malta, enjoying the finest meals one could ask for, a large assortment of new clothing and the most excellent accommodations on the island. With their continuing passage to Rome having been arranged and fully paid by the exceptionally grateful Maltese folks, they had no obligations for ninety days. Many started each day with a brisk walk around the estate, followed by a satisfying breakfast. After breakfast all who endured the storm aboard Shanesse without exception resolutely met to hear Paul's words. Having a clear understanding that their current situation was solely to the credit of Paul, they also understood that they each owed him their very lives. Joined by many locals, they intently listened to Paul's teaching, convinced that they would remain citizens of God's Kingdom regardless of future events.

Walking into the large hall for the morning gathering, Publius recalled that day in the cold rain only one month ago that he was traveling out to see Paul at the site of the wreck. He specifically remembered thinking... What an enormous impact this will have on the island. One of the gods walking and talking with us right here on Malta. Things will never be the same.... He understood now that Paul was not a god, but no one could have imagined how dramatically things were going to change. Paul certainly represented the One True God well, he thought, teaching continuously and sharing the good news of the Kingdom. In only thirty days, things had changed dramatically. Most apparent was the fact that no sick or diseased person remained among them. But most notable was the change in the atmosphere of this little island nation. From the slave to the wealthiest businessman, attitudes had changed. People were grateful to God for life and treated all with respect. The slaves worked more diligently than ever before and the owners began treating them with respect and dignity. Publius along with the other Maltese officials had publicly repented before God for their past which included liberating the cargo of many a distressed vessel that beached on their treacherous shores and taking its occupants as captives. Slaves publicly forgave their captors and many were offered their freedom by their masters. One incredible turn of events was the fact that few slaves were accepting their freedom, choosing rather to stay right here in Malta with their masters as bond servants. The big issue now was getting the day's work completed in time to go to Publius' estate for the afternoon meetings.

In the afternoons the islanders, having completed their work for the day, would flock to Publius' estate. Paul reasoned with the well-informed, highly educated, cultured individuals of Malta in Publius' smaller but very elegant conference hall. The hall was normally reserved exclusively for meetings with dignitaries. This group was not comprised specifically of dignitaries but many of these remarkably wealthy individuals had moved to Malta from every corner of the civilized world. Malta was very attractive and businessmen that frequented the area often returned with their families for their retirement years. The afternoon demand was so great, that Luke and Aristarchus also had meetings. In one adjoining building Luke taught the physicians, who currently had no work, and the other local professional people extensively on the life of Jesus, His incredible miracles and how to be led by the Spirit in their places of business. Aristarchus on the other hand, met with the commoners who packed the large meeting hall each afternoon. Over the last thirty days he had, much to their surprise, taught that they too could live powerful victorious lives. He assured them that the awesome opportunity of personally communing with the King of kings was open to them, even if they were slaves. And, he expounded on the tremendous importance and the incredible responsibility of being a mighty warrior, boldly representing the Kingdom of God. Aristarchus explained how these warrior's weapons of war are not swords and spears that can be seen. They war against principalities and powers, boldly pulling down strongholds.

"Your mandate is to protect Malta's borders and even control the heavens above. Never let your life as a slave or commoner hinder your service as a warrior for the Kingdom!" Aristarchus shouted. Then with everyone's full attention he told an incredible story of a young slave in a foreign country. "This slave," he said, "looked to the One True God for his wisdom, and his master soon recognized the fact that all he set his hand to prospered. This master was no ordinary man. He was a wealthy government official with many servants and slaves. But to his great satisfaction, he recognized the immense potential of this particular slave and placed his entire estate under the control of this very special young man." Pausing and looking across this large group he asked, "Do you realize what set this young man apart from all the other servants and slaves?" Waiting a moment for them to consider his question he continued, "Yes, his love for and connection to the One True God." Then with a very powerful voice he proclaimed, "The same God you're in covenant with, sealed with the blood of Jesus! And I don't have to explain covenant to you. You fully realize and understand that a blood covenant is the strongest agreement known to man. This covenant cannot be broken!" Then in earnest he continued, "So you see with the

help and favor of his God this slave rose to the very
pinnacle of authority in his master's house,
controlling everything that he owned. Generating
no small profit for him, his master recognized the
fact that his entire household and even his fields
were prospering greatly because of this young man.
This master was so confident in his slave's abilities
and so pleased with his results that the only thing he
personally cared about was the bread that he ate."
Again pausing for the people to catch hold of what
he said, he looked out over everyone sitting there in
the hall, slaves, commoners and servants in their
own eyes but a precious and powerful force to be
reckoned with in God's eyes. Nodding with sincere
approval he quietly said, "You are very important;
never underestimate your worth. Not only can you
protect this island of Malta as mighty warriors of the
Kingdom of God, you can change it in the natural
and bring great blessing and prosperity on this land,
on those you work for and those you work with."
Pausing for a moment, tears came to his eyes as he
looked out over these precious people. Trying to
find his voice, he encouraged them repeating,
"Never underestimate your worth, you are," and he
stopped for a second, again trying to find his voice,
then continued, "very, very important!" he said
insistently.

Taking a drink of water, Aristarchus continued.
"Listen to me carefully my friends, I am not

promising you an easy life. I can assure you a victorious life if you completely give yourself to the One True God that we continually speak of, but I cannot promise you a life of ease by any stretch of the mind's eye. It was a very hard difficult road for that young slave that I told you about, but we all like the part where he's risen to the very pinnacle of authority in his master's house don't we? This young man that we are so pleased with was not born a slave. He was born into a very wealthy Hebrew family and was taught about the One True God from childhood. His true life story is recorded in the Torah, the Hebrew Bible. With eleven brothers and many sisters, what went so terribly wrong? How did this young man end up being a slave? None of his siblings were slaves. Consider his life," Aristarchus said. "Would you continue to trust God and do your best if your mother died when you were very young; your own brothers decided to kill you but at the last moment secretly sold you into slavery? Your brothers tell your father who loves you, that you were killed by a wild animal. So instead of trying to find you, your loving father has a funeral in your memory and mourns on your behalf. After all that you arrive as a slave in a distant country where they serve false gods and idols. How are you going to cope with this unpleasant situation? You can't even understand your master's words. You must first learn a new language so you can obey his requests. It no longer looks easy, does it? Can you expect the One True God whom you serve to bless this heathen master of yours? But God remained with this young slave as he walked through these difficult times. As a slave he ascended to a position of authority bringing prosperity to his master. In turn, he was placed in the honorable position of directing and overseeing this important government official's entire estate, sure it was worth the effort, right?

"Or, what about my situation?" Aristarchus asked. "I endured fourteen of the most grueling days of my life, living in clothing saturated with blood, waste and vomit. I literally had the life slowly beaten out of me aboard Shanesse in that Nor'easter. I can't even describe those days to you. I was sicker than I thought a man could get and was convinced we were all going to die. But here I am, with the privilege of introducing many of you to Jesus and teaching the good news of the Kingdom. Was it worth it? Without a doubt! My point being, it's not always easy, but it's worth it, and I've found over the years, the greater the test, the greater the reward.

"As I said, the story of the young slave is a true story, recorded in the Torah. The young slave's name was Joseph and his master was Potiphar, but the story doesn't end with Joseph being highly esteemed and Potiphar being blessed. Potiphar's wife greatly admired their young handsome slave. She realized that he had brought great blessing to their entire household. Now she was convinced that the only thing that could be better, would be if she could secretly get in bed with him. One day she very directly asks him if he will join her in bed.

"He clearly states, 'After Potiphar has withheld nothing of his from me except you his wife, how could I do this great wickedness and sin against God?

"She has no concern for Potiphar or sin and says, 'It will be our secret'. Joseph honorably refuses her request but day after day she longingly persists with her invitations.

"One day, Joseph accidentally finds himself in the house alone with her. What a mistake, Potiphar's shameless little wife grabbed his clothing and said, 'Lay with me!' Leaving his garment in her hands he ran out of the house. This irritated her so severely that she told Potiphar when he returned that Joseph tried to get in bed with her. Proving her accusation holding Joseph's clothing in her hands she said, 'I narrowly escaped but when I shouted for help, Joseph fled.' Potiphar promptly had Joseph placed in prison.

"Now think of yourself in this situation, what are you going to do, is it still worth it?" Aristarchus asked. "You didn't commit a crime; you're actually in prison for protecting someone else's interests.

But the only person who knows the truth is your accuser, and no one else can be bothered with your version of the story. You're as low on the social scale as one can get. You're a foreign slave in the king's prison for molesting a high ranking government official's wife." Stopping and looking closely at the people Aristarchus stressed, "But this was no ordinary high ranking government official, Potiphar was the captain of the royal guard." Again stopping and looking at the wide eyed people, who were realizing the critical state that Joseph had found himself in, he further emphasized. "But Potiphar was not only the captain of the royal guard, he was also the chief executioner!" Aristarchus quietly stated, "It would be best to take what you have coming very quietly, no words, because the blink of an eye could get you killed right now."

A few quiet gasps were heard throughout the crowd, confirming they knew exactly what he was talking about.

"Yes," Aristarchus went on, "and everyone knows how human nature seems to believe that as one climbs the ladder of success, he no longer has to live by the same code that was necessary when he was a nobody. It's easy for people to believe that a mere slave, having been highly esteemed and given charge of menservants, maidservants, household affairs and business affairs could get off track. This slave, directing everything and everybody on a luxurious estate, handling large sums of money and making important decisions, with everything going his way, could easily overestimate his privileges with his master's wife."

Again Aristarchus asked, "In Joseph's circumstances, what are you going to do? You worked so hard, for so many years, poured out your heart and soul for your master, overcame great obstacles and greatly improved your master's holdings, all the time being completely honest and upright. Your reward is a small cell in the king's prison with death lingering nearby." Aristarchus quietly asked, "In Joseph's situation, what can you do?"

The people were very quiet. Their faces visibly showed they could feel Joseph's pain. Aristarchus spoke firmly as he continued. "Don't forget the most important factor in this true life story. Joseph not only served Potiphar, he served the One True God. God was with Joseph in prison, showed him mercy and gave him favor. In a short while the prison keeper placed Joseph in charge of all the prisoners. The prison keeper didn't look into anything that was under Joseph's authority. Does this sound familiar?" asked Aristarchus. "All that Joseph did was made to prosper because the One True God was with him!

"The king, or ruler of Egypt was called Pharaoh," Aristarchus continued, "and Pharaoh was disgruntled with his chief butler and his chief baker so he placed them in prison where they were of course under Joseph's care. One day Joseph noticed that they were very agitated and unsettled about something. Asking them what was worrying them, he found that they each had a dream and were very concerned about its interpretation. Joseph said interpretations belong to God and asked them to tell him the dreams. The butler explained his dream to Joseph with the hope that maybe he could shed a bit of light on its meaning. God gave Joseph the interpretation and he in turn, explained to the butler that in three days he would be restored to his position of chief butler and again serve Pharaoh. Joseph went on to ask the butler to remember him, and tell Pharaoh about him being wrongly imprisoned. The butler gladly agreed to bring Joseph's situation to Pharaoh's attention, having received the wonderful news of getting out of prison himself.

"Seeing that the interpretation for the butler was positive, the baker also told Joseph his dream. Joseph told the baker that in three days, Pharaoh would take his head from him and hang his body from a tree and the birds would come and eat his flesh." Aristarchus said, "I'm guessing that the baker tried to put those words out of his mind, reasoning that Joseph was only a crazy Hebrew slave, foolish enough to mess with the executioner's wife! How brainless is that!" Aristarchus continued, "But in three days it was Pharaoh's birthday and he called for the chief butler and the chief baker. News came back to the prison, that the interpretations were absolutely accurate and exactly what Joseph said, happened.

"This, I'm sure, was very exciting for Joseph as he realized the fact that not only was the butler going to tell Pharaoh about him being wrongfully imprisoned, he would surely also mention the fact that Joseph interpreted both dreams with one hundred percent accuracy. This should get Pharaoh's attention enough to at least review his case! In anticipation, Joseph waited to hear from Pharaoh. The end of the day came and no word from Pharaoh. It's his birthday, Joseph reasoned, surely tomorrow when the festivities settle down, I'll hear from Pharaoh. The following day came and went, no word. Pharaoh may have had a lot of work to catch up on since he took yesterday off for his birthday, surely tomorrow I'll hear from him. A full week came and went. Joseph must have thought, I'm sure Pharaoh is an exceptionally busy man, ruling the nation and everything, maybe the butler will come with some news for me. Surely the butler would be grateful enough to bring me word. A month came and went, nothing! Now Joseph was thinking, maybe the chief butler will just send a messenger since he is also apparently very busy.

Two full years came and went, Joseph had long since realized that the butler had forgotten about him." Aristarchus again asked, "Is it worth keeping on, when you operate flawlessly in your God given gifts and no one recognizes you? What about when even those who greatly benefited from your God given gift, simply forget you even exist?

"Then one day much to Joseph's surprise he received word. Pharaoh wanted to see him! Joseph cleaned up, shaved, put on his best clothing and was brought before Pharaoh. Much to his surprise, this meeting had nothing to do with justice. It had nothing to do with being framed and wrongfully imprisoned. The Pharaoh wasn't interested in Joseph or his problems at all. Pharaoh had a dream and no one could interpret it. He was only interested in the interpretation of his dream. The butler had told Pharaoh that Joseph could interpret dreams and apparently that was all he told him. So what's going to happen, interpret the dream for Pharaoh and go back to prison?" Looking at the people Aristarchus asked, "Is it worth doing your best even if there's no benefit whatsoever in it for you?" Some nodded but others were not convinced. They were disgusted at the injustice that Joseph faced for such a long time as he did his best to be faithful to the One True God.

Aristarchus continued. "Joseph told the Pharaoh in no uncertain terms that his God was the one who held the secret of the dream." "Notice," Aristarchus pointed out, "he's not trying to establish himself, but instead he's giving full credit to his God. Remember when Potiphar's wife tried to seduce Joseph, his reply was that he wouldn't sin against his God." "Think about it," Aristarchus persisted. "He didn't quietly tell Mrs. Potiphar, we can't do that because someone might find out. He boldly said he would not sin against his God. Now standing before Pharaoh, you notice that Joseph didn't say, 'I'll tell you the dream if you'll get me out of prison.' What he did say was, 'My God will give you a favorable answer of peace'.

"What happened next shows us clearly how our God can turn things around for those who have only one purpose and that being to live for the One True God. Pharaoh told Joseph two dreams and Joseph not only interpreted them but also laid out a plan for Pharaoh that would save his people from starvation. Pharaoh was that impressed with Joseph and his God that he immediately placed Joseph in the position of top commander of the nation, second only to Pharaoh himself. The shower and shave with his best clothing from the prison no longer measured up." With much emotion Aristarchus loudly continued, "Joseph was dressed up in a royal robe of fine linen. The signet ring of Pharaoh placed on his finger. A gold chain placed around his neck and was driven through the city in

Pharaoh's own chariot with criers going before him shouting 'Bow the Knee'!"

Settling down a bit Aristarchus continued, "After thirteen years of difficulty, persistently doing his very best, Joseph found himself as low as a human being could go on the social scale, a Hebrew slave in an Egyptian prison, overlooked and forgotten." "But in one day," he shouted, "The One True God promoted Joseph from a forgotten slave in prison to second in command of Egypt, the most prominent nation of the world in Joseph's day! Was It Worth It? Was it worth choosing what was right in the face of great adversity?

"If you don't have something worth dying for, life isn't worth living. Our King and His Kingdom are worth dying for, and this gives great value to the life that we live right now. Never underestimate your worth my friends. Allow the One True God to establish you! Your mandate is to protect Malta's borders and even control the heavens above, whether in the spirit world or the natural world. Never let your life as a slave or commoner hinder your service for the Kingdom!" Aristarchus concluded.

No longer seeing themselves as persons of little value, that group of servants, slaves and commoners left the building walking tall with a great resolve to honorably represent their King the One True God at all costs, allowing their God to establish them in his

Kingdom where the Commander In Chief is the servant of all. ☞

Chapter 13

The Life They Once Knew

༄

As the ship quietly slipped into the Ostia harbor, the sun was setting in the west leaving a most incredible sky filled with shades of crimson. The sky brought tears to Nassor's eyes as it reminded him of Jesus' blood and His sacrifice for us. What an astonishing few months it had been. Never before had life been so precious and it seemed that people had become much more important to him. Each person representing his own set of circumstances, husbands, wives, families, communities, all linked together in different ways, but each important to the other. Even though precious few of them seemed to realize the connection, being so wrapped up in their own person that they barely recognized the other even existed.

I too must have changed Nassor thought, only a few months ago I was willing to sacrifice a shipload of people to escape with my life. Now I see these same people so precious that I would like to accompany each of them home, just so I could continually remind them of what Jesus did for them. This must be what Paul spoke of as we sat for hours and listened to his words about having died to our old selves. It was incredible to watch everyone from our ship gladly accept Jesus as their Savior back on the island of Malta, but how quickly they forget. Then, having just come through that dreadful storm, watching everyone get healed, and listening to Paul's words for three months with no place to go and no commitments, it made perfect sense to allow Jesus first place in their lives. But now, arriving at their desired destination months later than they expected, with commitments and obligations, it seemed like many had already forgotten their commitment to remain citizens of God's Kingdom, regardless of future events. Nassor had spent a lot of his free time in the passengers' quarters on this short trip. Many friendships had been established on Malta. His growing concern was how the smooth sailing and the calm weather seemed to lull the passengers, his friends, back into complacency. Their conversations had been slowly turning from the things of the Lord back to all the regular bits and pieces.

Being quite busy, Nassor's attention returned to the task at hand as he secured mooring lines to the starboard side.

Nassor said, "What do you think Mecho man? Sailing quietly right up to the dock, we're not used to that."

Mecho who was working with him said, "Isn't that a switch, but I'm fairly convinced that this little gift from God will basically go unnoticed. Many of our people have prayed that we won't have to anchor off and wait a few days for a light breeze to move our ship up to the dock and this evening, conditions couldn't be better. But most of them are missing the point. Their focus has turned from God to schedules and things."

"Yeah," Nassor said, "Please Lord, I lost all my stuff, please Lord, I'm months behind with my schedule. That seems to be the focus of the prayer meetings. Last evening after dinner I stopped the entire group I was with and asked, what is so important that you could just forget? They looked at me like I didn't understand. I wanted to shout at them, People, People, People! Don't go back to your old ways just because you're back to familiar places. Mecho, I'm worried about them. When we get off the ship tomorrow, they will all be going their own way, but how many will be carriers of the light? How many will remember that their lives were saved for a reason and how many will fall right back into their old ways?"

"Your lines ready?" Ulray shouted from the stern.

"Good up here," Mecho shouted back.

With only a few hundred yards to go, all the sails with the exception of one small head sail were dropped and neatly lashed to the yards. Nassor stood ready on the bow with a small hand line to throw to the dock hands as soon as Twin Brothers moved close enough. The end of the small hand line was tied to one of the large mooring lines that was secured to the ship. The dock hands would pull the large mooring line to the dock and attach it to the big supporting timbers, securing Twin Brothers to the dock. The ship was named after Zeus' sons, the twin brothers Castor and Pollux. It was a well built vessel but those who boarded the Twin Brothers in Malta had lost the deep respect they had for the gods, after sitting under Paul, Aristarchus and Luke's teaching for three months. Most of the sailors from Shanesse were anxious to arrive in port to find positions on other boats but Jag, Ulray, Mecho and Nassor were offered positions on the Twin Brothers the moment they came aboard. Capt.

Warnken gave them high recommendations back on Malta and even though Twin Brothers was already crewed, they secured paying positions for the trip back to Rome with the option of permanent employment.

"They better be dropping that headsail real soon or we'll be scraping some paint off the Twins," Nassor said quietly to Mecho who stood ready by his side.

Mecho replied, "You could search a very long time to find a Captain even half as good as Capt. Warnken. And you're right, they should have already dropped that headsail."

Finally the order went out and the headsail was dropped.

"We're carrying too much speed!" Nassor said quietly, "The helmsman better be the best there is or something's going to crunch."

Mecho laughed, "We don't want to bust old Castor's nose now do we?"

"The dock master isn't going to be pleased with us," Nassor said. "If we do manage to get this thing stopped, we're going to put a tremendous strain on their pilings."

"Be ready Ulray," Mecho shouted.

"We ready back here," Jag shouted back.

Jag was now amidships and Ulray was aft. They both recognized the problem and were prepared to time their line toss with Nassor up in the bow so they could simultaneously load three dock lines, greatly improving their chances of salvaging this misjudged approach without damaging the Twin Brothers or the dock. The helmsman steered hard to Port and then oversteered back to starboard in his efforts to slow down, but all he accomplished was a strange approach angle. Now there was no way Jag and Ulray could reach the dock with their lines. Throwing the two forward lines, Nassor and Mecho looked at each other knowing trouble was near. By now the dock master was shouting, the helmsman was shouting, Twin Brothers inexperienced Captain Gracchus was shouting and the front mooring lines came tight. Everything happened in extreme slow motion. The lines strained, the dock strained and creaked, the Twin Brothers slowly continued on, swinging to starboard. Slowly creaking and crunching its way ahead, Castor and Pollux faced a huge timber and neither the figurehead nor the timber came out looking good when the Twin Brothers finally stopped.

"I guess it goes without saying," Nassor said, "You can't stop a few hundred tons on a Denarius."

Looking at Nassor, Mecho said, "Now there you have the classic example of inexperience. The perfect evening, the perfect breeze and-"

He stopped short as Captain Gracchus came forward to evaluate the damages. With long loud bursts of profanities, the captain and the dock master exchanged their views of the problem at hand. A small skiff came alongside the stern and received the lines from Jag and Ulray. Rowing over to the dock, they passed them to the dockworkers who slowly worked the ship into position by the dock.

With the gang plank in place, Nassor, Mecho, Jag and Ulray made their way off the Twin Brothers and onto the dock to survey the damages. There was no serious structural damage to the ship but the dock would require quite a few gold pieces to rectify it from this evening's events.

Quietly, making sure no one else could hear, Mecho said, "We did break old Castor's nose, didn't we?"

Jag laughed quietly and said, "Those two unfortunate gods look as if they met the One True God this evening, don't they?"

With night quickly approaching, Captain Gracchus placed three armed men on watch and ordered everyone to remain aboard until first light, which was not at all out of line as the docks were not known as the safest place in Ostia after dark. One could literally find the admirable, the terrible and the revolting inhabitants of Ostia milling around the dock during the day. The trouble was that after dark, the admirable retired to their homes and only the terrible and the revolting individuals remained.

Captain Warnken, Benjobo, Nassor, Jag, Ulray and Mecho visited with Paul, Luke and Aristarchus until the early hours of the morning. Jag, Ulray and Benjobo had made a decision for Jesus a few days after Captain and Nassor had joined Mecho who led the way. They spoke of the things of the Kingdom and Paul encouraged them in many ways. None of them were at all pleased about Paul going to Rome as a prisoner and did not really understand why it had to be that way. Paul seemed fine with it, having explained to them many times that he was a prisoner of the Lord Jesus Christ, not a prisoner of Rome. Paul laid hands on Benjobo and prophesied.

"You have a very important decision to make. It will ultimately determine life or death for you. Pray about it my friend; you need to hear God on this one."

Benjobo was very quiet, and retired to his quarters early.

Laying hands on Captain Warnken Paul prophesied. "I see you planting churches in many places that you're already familiar with as you have traveled there in the past."

Prophesying over Nassor he said, "Nassor, your name means 'victorious warrior'. Be bold, be strong and be very courageous, the Lord Your God is with you. I see a pure heart with deep love and compassion for people, but I also see a ferocious warrior for the Kingdom. Your strength and strategy will come from your personal time with the Lord."

Prophesying over Mecho he said, "You're a teacher, Mecho. I see a powerful teacher promoting the kingdom in simple, even a bit rough around the edges, sailor-style, but very effective as you can reach many that others can't."

Paul then reached out and touched Jag and he fell to the floor like a lifeless body. Paul said, "Jag I see you sailing the seas and at the same time carrying a powerful witness, a light for the Kingdom."

"Ulray," Paul said, laying hands on him, "I see an encourager spreading the good news of the Kingdom. Don't let outside influence sway your resolve for the King and His Kingdom."

The night being well spent, they all retired to their quarters.

Early the following morning the docks were already alive with activity. There were many goodbyes as people left the ship. Their time on Shanesse followed by three months on Malta had taken two hundred and seventy six strangers and molded many friendships. Many of the people were eager to visit with loved ones in Rome who had expected them to arrive last fall, not this spring. Not terribly enthusiastic about sailing with Captain Gracchus aboard the Twin Brothers, Nassor and Mecho collected their wages and joined Paul who of course was led by Julius the centurion. The group included the detachment of soldiers, the other prisoners and of course Luke and Aristarchus. Having taken leave of their good friends Jag, Ulray and Capt. Warnken, Nassor and Mecho left the docks that were situated in the beautiful mouth of the Tiber River and led the whole entourage northeast through Ostia. This port city of Rome was beautiful. Nassor and Mecho familiar with the region acted as tour guides, pointing out the attractions as they passed many sculptures and mosaics. They highly recommended the Thermopolium for lunch, so the entire group stopped at this upscale eatery which had a marble countertop bar and a large fresco. The fresco, a plaster wall that had been painted while the plaster was still wet, permanently pictured fruits, vegetables and other food specialties that were sold in the Thermopolium. After lunch they passed the House of Diana which was near the Forum Square where the public debates were held and on the other side of the Forum Square, Nassor pointed out the huge thermal baths.

"The sailors could hardly wait to come out here to these huge warm baths in the evenings and the parties were..." Nassor's voice faded away and he paused for a moment. Finally he continued, "I wouldn't recommend the evening dinner parties."

Mecho took over saying, "It's easy to recognize the fact that not only does a great deal of money pass through this port city, quite a bit stays here. Up ahead is the Basilica. You see the Roman style columned aisles on each side? The inside is shaped in a semicircle. They use that building for a court of justice. I spent one very unpleasant day in there. Probably would have ended up in prison if Capt. Warnken wouldn't have come to my rescue and promised the officials we'd set sail that same day. I'm told things got a little out of hand at the dinner party at the baths the night before. I personally don't remember the evening at all; I only remember the next day in court and a pounding headache." Continuing Mecho said, "Just ahead we see the Temple of Rome and the black and white mosaics representing Neptune."

Preparing to leave Ostia and travel up the Tiber River by barge Nassor said, "We often travel by the sea road from here to Rome but we always return by barge as the trip down the Tiber River is quick and easy compared to being towed up the river."

At the edge of town as the barge was being loaded and their group was boarding, they met

Benjobo being led away by the lanista. Sure that Benjobo had made a huge mistake, Nassor tried to negotiate for his freedom only to find that Benjobo pledged his allegiance even before he was purchased.

Benjobo explained his reasoning to Nassor, "Watching Paul being led out of town as a prisoner, I have lost confidence in Paul's God." Benjobo said, "I watched Paul do the impossible aboard Shanesse as he rallied the people's hope and got them all safely ashore just as he promised. I saw Paul survive a Naja haje bite with no ill effects. I personally witnessed signs and wondrous miracles as we all watched Paul heal all the sick on the island of Malta. I saw favor come to all who were aboard Shanesse as their food lodging and passage aboard the Twin Brothers was graciously taken care of. After seeing all of those things that Paul did for his God. How can I serve Paul's God who rewards him with prison?" Benjobo asked. "Paul has been wholly dedicated to his God who seemed so loving and compassionate to others and even so, Paul's being led off to prison! I'm familiar with Rome," Benjobo continued insistently. "As a prisoner in Rome, Paul will very likely end up being a spectacle of the games in the coliseum. I've been to the games many times in the past and will at all costs avoid the opportunity to participate as a prisoner. A prisoner's part in the games is to entertain the people by facing the lions unarmed. Do you remember Paul's words to me last night? He said that I have a decision to make, and my life depends on it. I choose to live as a gladiator and not die as a prisoner. I will be armed and trained for my encounter in the coliseum; Paul will face the lions unarmed and alone. I will earn back my dignity, fame and wealth as a master of the games; Paul will die as a prisoner. I am confident with my decision. I have no other choice, I lost everything."

The reality of this difficult situation was suddenly clear to Nassor. Paul was being led off to Rome completely dependent upon his God to defend him, while Benjobo was being led off to Rome completely dependent upon his skills to defend him. Nassor watched the lanista lead Benjobo off to be branded.

Arriving in Rome, Paul was granted the freedom to stay in a home of his own at his expense. Paul rented a very nice house in a good section of the city with only a small portion of the great wealth that he was given in Malta. He arranged meetings with everyone from the dignitaries of Roman to the leaders of the local Jewish community. Nassor and Mecho helped Paul with many things as he was

confined to his own home and could not travel at all, while Luke and Aristarchus helped him teach the scores of people that continuously came and went.
ᕊ

Chapter 14

Freed by a Prisoner

꒦

Beryl traveled to Rome.   Making his way through the city, he was looking for the specific address he was given by the messenger. This is quite a wealthy section of the city he said to himself as he neared his destination, and that's saying something when you're in Rome he thought. Coming up to the house, he was met by a servant who took care of his horse and wagon.   Another showed him to the door that was guarded by two armed guards. I've made some furniture for men of great wealth but this is impressive he thought as the guards stepped aside allowing him and the servant to enter.

A man appeared in the hallway, walking up to him he said, "Hello Beryl, the Lord told me your heart is heavy because you exposed your little girl."

Very taken aback, Beryl was not impressed with this harsh introduction. He thought of turning and walking out. Who does this man think he is, insulting me like that? Of course he knows my name, Beryl reasoned. His messenger was in my shop, and as far as exposing my daughter, there are probably not a dozen men in the city of Rome who haven't exposed a daughter. Quickly developing a very bad attitude Beryl decided he didn't have to take this abuse from anyone, no matter how rich they were and turned to leave.

The man continued, "She looked just like your oldest daughter and you've been having bad dreams ever since. You keep hearing her cry, 'recognize me daddy'."

Falling to his knees, completely broken Beryl said, "Stop, please stop," and began sobbing uncontrollably.

Walking up behind him, the man put his hands on Beryl's shoulders and said, "The One True God knows you by name and has seen all you have ever done but still loves you. He sent His only Son, Jesus the Christ to take away your guilt and your sorrows. There is forgiveness and new life for all those who accept Jesus the Christ as their Lord and Savior."

Beryl whispered between sobs, "Please forgive me Jesus, Please forgive me, I accept You as my Lord." It was as if a bolt of lightning shot through Beryl's entire being, he felt extreme heat and he collapsed on the floor.

Nearly an hour went by before Beryl stirred. Two men helped him to a couch where he relaxed while he tried to understand what had just happened. The man he met when he arrived came over and sat down beside him.

"Beryl, my name is Paul. Luke and Aristarchus are the men who helped you up in the hallway. You just met the Lord God Almighty, the One True God. Your sins are forgiven, and I want you to know that your little baby girl is not dead but alive and doing fine, living with our King and Lord. When our bodies can no longer survive here on earth and they fall down dead, all who have accepted Jesus as their Lord as you have, simply go to live with Him. You will see your daughter again and will spend eternity together with her and your Lord Jesus."

Beryl was not sure he understood everything Paul was telling him but he was sure of one thing, he believed every word of it! Those were the kindest words he had ever heard. He just had the scariest, and at the same time the most exhilarating experience of his life and he truly felt like a new man. "Paul, how did you know all those things about me?" Beryl asked. "I only ever told my closest friend about my bad dreams, and I never told anyone about my little girl looking like Odilia, my oldest daughter."

Paul replied, "The Lord our God shows me things and I say what I see and hear from Him."

Beryl accepted Paul's invitation to stay for lunch and discuss his furniture needs after a good meal. The meal was ready to be served as Paul and Beryl joined at least twenty five other people in the dining hall. Reclining at the table Beryl noticed that there was an assortment of furnishings, none of which matched. He figured that may be why he was here. Feeling a bit out of place, he also noted that many of the guests appeared to be dignitaries or other very influential persons. Who is this Paul? Beryl quietly questioned in his thoughts as he considered the day's events. He says he represents the One True God, and I believe him. No one else could know the things that he knows. As Beryl began to eat he started to shake. Not now he thought, but his hands quivered violently. Completely embarrassed, Beryl folded them in his lap until they finally stopped shaking and he could finish his meal. After lunch, Paul discussed the furniture he needed and gave Beryl a substantial order with three hundred gold pieces as a deposit. Paul actually wanted custom furniture for many rooms of his house, not just the dining room and Beryl's expanded shop could easily handle an order like this.

"Just out of curiosity," Beryl asked, "how did you learn about my furniture shop? Did your God tell you that too?"

Paul smiled and said, "Some friends of mine are Roman nobility, and they highly recommended you. They said they placed an order through a friend of theirs who owns a linen shop. They were more than pleased when they received their furnishings from you last year and claim that with everyday use, as they continuously entertain important officials that arrive on government business, your furniture is holding up far better than expected. That my friend is why I contacted you, but as we now understand our Lord also wanted to visit with you. I have classes here nearly every day; three of us teach of the Kingdom of the Lord Jesus Christ. It would be very beneficial if you could join us for a few classes, as this will help you understand the things of God."

Beryl, gladly accepting Paul's generous invitation said, "I would be honored to join you when I return with your furniture."

"We will be looking forward to seeing you then, my friend," Paul replied. "And today before you leave, Luke will explain some important things to you about serving our Lord. Now I must go. Our guests that you met during lunch are here for some teaching also. It's very nice to get to know you, Beryl," Paul said shaking his hand. Pointing in

Luke's direction he added, "there's Luke. He will want to spend a bit of time with you before you go. Thanks again for coming out to see me. I can't travel right now; I'm confined to this house."

Questioning his last statement Beryl thought, he looks healthy why would he be confined to his house? Smiling, Beryl thanked Paul many times and turned to find Luke.

Beryl recognized Luke, as he was the one reclining next to him at the lunch meal. Luke very patiently explained the basics of the Kingdom to Beryl over the next two hours, answering many questions and pointing him in the right way regarding some basic issues of life.

Beryl said, "Luke I don't know everything that happened when I met Jesus today but I know He forgave my sins. For the first time, I feel that I can live with myself after having exposed our daughter. I hope my wife, Apphia, can forgive me also." Just for a moment Beryl began to shake again.

Luke said, "Beryl, I'm a physician; you seem to be having some difficulty. I noticed you had trouble at lunch also. Has this been bothering you for awhile now?"

Feeling like he could tell Luke anything without being condemned he said, "I don't know what it is; it's been getting worse and worse. I used to enjoy carving finely detailed things but I get part way through my work and promptly destroy it when I suddenly start shaking. It's been very frustrating."

"Have you been taking any medication for it?" Luke asked.

"No," Beryl said, "I wouldn't know what to take, and I haven't seen a doctor." Thinking of his elixir of sleep he added, "I have been taking something to help me sleep. It's been difficult for me with the bad dreams about my daughter."

"What have you been taking?" Luke asked. Beryl produced a small bottle of his elixir of sleep and showed it to Luke, he carried it with him perchance he needed to spend the night.

"Henbane," Luke read the label aloud. "This 'elixir of sleep' as you call it will help you sleep, but it's poison to your system if you take too much of it. It should be used sparingly and only on rare occasion, usually for extreme instances when your body desperately needs rest." Looking at Beryl he asked, "Have you been using this regularly?"

Nodding his head Beryl said, "Shendo, the man who I buy my fabric from, gave me some when I hadn't slept but a few hours in a few weeks, and he told me not to use it regularly, but it worked so well that I used it nearly every day for most of a year now."

Luke looked at him very seriously and said, "Beryl, this stuff is poisoning your system. This extract comes from a plant of the nightshade family;

scopolamine is the active ingredient. That stuff is dangerous, and I believe your body is addicted to it. Scopolamine is not only used in small doses for helping someone sleep, it's also used to prevent seasickness. In larger doses it's used as a truth serum and will cause amnesia. In other words, when under its influence a person will not hesitate to answer questions that expose the secrets of his heart and have no recollection of having done so when he wakes. But the big problem remains, it is a poison and your body is currently saturated with it. You must stop using it immediately! It's very important my friend; you must not use this elixir anymore," Luke emphasized. "Drink a lot of water, eat fresh fruit and vegetables and get plenty of rest. That would be the natural remedy, but you will find as you walk the walk of life in the Kingdom, the spirit of a man brings life to his mortal body. Your step of faith in the Lord Jesus Christ is the key to beating this addiction. I'll pray specifically for you my friend. But I want you to realize that even if it's difficult, you will make it. Combine the natural remedy with faith in the spiritual and you will succeed!"

After praying together, Beryl was on his way back home with plenty to think about, the largest furniture order he ever received and three hundred pieces of gold being his smallest point of awareness. Fascinating...he contemplated. The last time I was sure I found the answer to my difficulties. A large furniture order, a bag of gold and a bottle of elixir seemed to be the solution. My business grew spectacularly, Shendo helped me in every way he knew, and I made more money than I ever did in my life. Simultaneously, I fell deeper and deeper into despair realizing that I could have paid another dowry. There actually was another way. I didn't have to expose my daughter, hurt my wonderful wife, devastate my dear Odilia and become addicted to a poison that's destroying my body! What an answer, it certainly wasn't truth!

"Truth," he blurted aloud, "I've been taking a truth serum!"

Beryl deliberated, what secrets of my heart have I boldly told people? I don't remember...of course you don't remember he thought. Luke said the medication also causes amnesia.

"All that and it's poison too," he said quietly as he pulled the little bottle of elixir out of his coat. "Elixir of sleep," he said with disgust. "It sure would be nice to see the big picture when an individual thinks he's found the truth."

Tossing the bottle high in the air he heard it break along the road behind him. Never looking back he said boldly, "I'll tell the truth without that poison, and I can sleep with the peace that Jesus gave me."

At that moment, his body began to shake violently as a reminder of his addiction. "Stop that," he shouted, and began praying to the One True God in the name of Jesus as Luke had taught him.

In a few minutes he stopped shaking but he did not stop praying, for the next two hours he spoke with his Lord and felt a renewed peaceful presence much like that morning when he met Jesus for the first time. Beryl prayed for Luke his new friend who shared such a wealth of truth with him this afternoon and for Paul, the great man of God who drove him to his knees within moments of entering his house.

Thinking of Paul, he had asked Luke why Paul said he was confined to his house. He looked healthy and fit enough to travel. Luke explained that Paul was a prisoner of the Empire of Rome, and that the guards posted at the front were not there specifically to guard Paul's great wealth, but had orders to confine him to his house. Luke made it clear that the guards really liked Paul and his whole staff and were amazed at the official dignitaries that came to hear his words. Paul told the guards that he would not leave the house and they had complete confidence in his words. They had become trusted friends and acted much more like personal body guards than prison keepers, looking out for Paul's interests and protecting him from malicious visitors. Beryl wondered, how could it be, a powerful man representing the One True God, a man who could see deep within ones heart, a man who spoke with the authority of the King, a man of great wealth and unparalleled integrity, a man with a profound love and deep compassion for others... a prisoner? What terrible crimes could he have committed?

At home Apphia was thinking of Beryl as she worked with some business customers, matching fabric samples from Shendo's shop with color samples from their home. She had samples of most of Shendo's fabric right here in their display area and spent much time doing what she enjoyed, amazing customers with the perfect fabrics for their project. They had a servant that looked after the children four hours each day, allowing Apphia to help with the business but she insisted on spending most of each day with her children. The girls needed to learn from their mother. Burrus, quite grown up at five years old, already spent a few hours a day in school, but he needed mother too.

Taking a break, she went into the house. Their one slave was cleaning in the shop and Francis was helping the other one prepare food in the kitchen. Burrus was in school and the two younger girls were playing outside. Picking up the feather duster, she went into the living room and dusted her way over to the shrine in the corner. Thinking of Beryl's secret disgust for the gods which she too had come to despise, she purposely dusted one over, trying her best to make it look like an accident just in case anyone saw it happen. Deeply satisfied, she picked up the broken pieces and disposed of them. For a moment she considered the remaining lares but decided she had better leave good enough alone. Dusting a bit more just to make sure her little project looked authentic, Apphia put the duster away and stopped by the kitchen for a quick snack as she answered a few questions about tomorrow's menu.

As she slowly returned to the shop, she pondered. How could she possibly help Beryl? He was showing signs of despair and would surely pay the ultimate price if he did not leave his elixir of sleep alone. That drug was destroying him. She often saw him try to hide his shaking and quivering hands when she was around. Apphia loved him and could not imagine how she could carry on single-handedly. But the fact remained, he needed some good peaceful rest and he was not able to get any rest without his elixir of sleep, which in turn seemed to be the very thing that was ruining his health. Thinking of last night, she felt fear rise up within her. Beryl was also losing his memory. She remembered thinking about it from time to time; Beryl used to remember everything. He could look at a customer's project and remember all the details. More recently he often asked Apphia uncomplicated questions as he simply could not recall the information. And that nasty elixir, or loose juice as she called it, made for some interesting conversation as he bared his soul, but Apphia now found it difficult to have a relaxed conversation with the man she loved. This morning's conversation was very complex as she had to remember which things he knew she knew and which things he was sure no one knew.

Frustrated she said aloud, "There must be an answer."

It was late in the evening when Apphia heard Beryl's wagon arrive. Coming into the house, Beryl went straight over to the shrine in the corner and surveying the lares he turned to Apphia and said, "One of the gods is missing."

Her heart was in her throat as she stammered for words. "Which one?" she ask with a quivering voice. How could he know, she thought. No one saw me this afternoon...I'm sure of it...but Beryl came in the door and marched straight over to the shrine. What is he going to do to me? He said he hated them. Was he just acting like he didn't remember anything about last night when I made him breakfast this morning? Sitting down, as her legs simply refused to support her right at the moment, Apphia feared the worst. Now what is he doing? She asked herself, as Beryl gathered all their gods together and walked out of the door into the night. Fear gripped her, making it impossible to rise and follow Beryl to see what he was doing. Her mind raced with thoughts of divorce, questions of how could he know, and reasoning that he was removing the gods from their house to protect them from her.

A loud pounding noise outside commanded her attention. A moment later the door burst open, and Beryl was back in the room. Looking around the dimly lit room he saw Apphia frozen in fear, sitting on a chair in the corner. "It was an accident," she exclaimed with a shaky voice. "I was dusting, and I broke the one god. It was an accident," she insisted and began to cry.

Turning toward her, Beryl began shaking violently. Apphia's thoughts turned to despair. Now he's completely losing control and he's going to die right here in the living room she thought. Beryl called out to God and began praying but he was not even looking towards the empty shrine.

By now Apphia was distraught and rushed into the bedroom. Retrieving his bottle of elixir she came to his aid helping him sit down. He ended his prayer in the name of Jesus as his shaking subsided and she quickly offered him his bottle of medication. He turned and embraced Apphia. She cried in his arms, completely confused and mentally exhausted. She was the one shaking now as she held his bottle of medication that she had brought to help him. She suddenly realized that his elixir was one of the things that he did not know she knew about.

Holding her in his arms with no words for what seemed like an hour, Apphia sensed a gentle caring attitude. She actually felt safe in his arms. As hard as she tried, she could not gather words to speak; she was still holding the secret bottle of elixir that she was not supposed to know about, and he was still gently holding her in his arms.

Beryl spoke, "The man I went to see in Rome today is a prisoner."

"What?" Apphia replied quickly. "Do you mean the whole day was wasted? That big order the messenger spoke of was just a hoax! How did you get into the prison to see him?"

Releasing his hold on Apphia, Beryl walked over to the door and picked up three sacks that he had apparently brought in unnoticed as he arrived. At the same time, Apphia quickly set the bottle of elixir on the floor by the leg of the chair hoping that it would go unnoticed and maybe that entire component of this evening's disaster would be overlooked.

Returning, Beryl dropped the three sacks on the floor by Apphia's feet with a heavy thud and sat with her again on the large chair that he had made years earlier, specifically for that reason, so they could both sit closely as they spoke of the day's events. Amidst the turmoil of difficulty since their last baby, this special chair had not been used at all. It is very nice to sit close with my Beryl again Apphia thought.

Kicking one of the sacks, Beryl said, "Three hundred gold coins for a deposit, the largest single order we ever received. The Prisoner's name is Paul."

Apphia asked, "What's a prisoner going to do with fine furniture?" Shaking her head in unbelief she continued, "Where are they going to put furniture of your quality in the dungeon?"

"Oh, he lives in his own house; it's very large and quite impressive," Beryl explained.

"But you just said he's a prisoner," Apphia replied. "Now you say he lives in his own house?"

"Yes," Beryl replied. "He's a prisoner and he lives in his own house."

Very confused, Apphia said without thinking, "This entire evening makes no sense whatsoever, are you sure you don't need -" and she stopped suddenly, not believing her own ears and having already reached for the bottle of elixir, she thought, what a foolish blunder. I wish I didn't know any of Beryl's secrets. They have already gotten me into more trouble than I could have imagined, and all of that in only one day.

Beryl said, "I don't want to use that stuff anymore. Luke the physician told me that medication has been poisoning my body. That's why I got the shakes."

Surprised, Apphia asked, "You were to see a doctor today?"

"Yes, Luke lives with Paul," Beryl said.

"Luke's a prisoner too?" Apphia said, "A doctor in prison, and these prisoners live in their own house and have lots of money. Beryl, you must be very tired, I believe you should get some sleep."

"Actually," Beryl said, "I'm not sleepy at all. I feel really good!"

"Then I'm sure I need some sleep," Apphia said. "I haven't understood anything that happened since you came home and took all the..." Again she stopped short, not believing she just brought up the missing god problem, and her heart again jumped up in her throat as she tensed up and tried to move away from Beryl just a bit. Why did I break that stupid god today? And how did Beryl know about it the moment he walked in the door? And how foolish can I be, every time things seem to start going good, I release my tongue and incriminating words flow. Did someone put some of Beryl's loose juice in my drink at the evening meal?

Recognizing that Apphia was completely confused, Beryl said, "If you're not too sleepy, why don't I start at the beginning and tell you about this incredible day. I met Jesus," he began.

"Does Jesus live with Paul and Luke?" Apphia asked, "Is he a prisoner too?"

"Yes, He lives with Paul and Luke," Beryl said, "But He's not a prisoner, He's a King!"

Very astonished Apphia said, "A king! A king lives with the prisoners?" Sitting up straight, wide eyed, Apphia was having a terrible time trying to connect with Beryl's story.

Beryl smiled, reached out and pulled her close with a big hug, and gently kissed her lips. Looking into her eyes he said "Apphia, I love you dearly. I made a terrible mistake not recognizing our daughter. I can only imagine how I must have hurt you, will you please forgive me?"

With a rush of tears Apphia nodded her head yes as again she plainly could not locate words. Beryl held her tightly and they cried together for a long while. Then Apphia whispered, "You are a good man Beryl, you're a good man." After sitting quietly for another few minutes, Apphia could not wait any longer. Sitting up straight she said, "Please tell me about your incredible day."

Smiling at his beautiful wife and enjoying her passionate excitement he thought, I have my Apphia back! She's a good wife; I wonder how many things I told her while taking that truth serum. She certainly knew where to find it. I didn't even know she knew I used the elixir.

Starting again Beryl said, "I'll try to explain my day as well as I can my lady, but you are going to have to wait with your questions just a bit for it to make any sense." Starting with his first five minutes meeting Paul he explained how this amazing man of the One True God knew his inmost secrets and drove him to his knees.

Beryl told Apphia what Paul said: "The One True God knows you by name and has seen all you have ever done but still loves you. He sent His only Son, Jesus the Christ to take away your guilt and your sorrows. There is forgiveness and new life for all those who accept Jesus the Christ as their Lord and Savior." Beryl said, "I asked Jesus to forgive me and accepted Him as my Lord, and it was as if a bolt of lightning shot through me and I fell on the floor. But I'm a different man now, and the first thing I wanted to do when I got home, was to remove the lares from our home. That's why I took them out and pounded them to dust. We now have the One True God, I don't want any other gods in our home.

Paying close attention to Beryl's words and recognizing the wonderful change in her husband, Apphia asked, "Can I too have Jesus as my Lord?"

Beryl led Apphia in prayer as Luke had taught him. Having asked Jesus for forgiveness, Apphia asked Beryl for forgiveness also. Beryl saw a sparkle in her eye that he had never seen before, she was so beautiful. Continuing the story of his day's events, Beryl told Apphia everything.

By now it was early morning, the sky was already getting light as they rose from the big chair. Beryl took the bottle of elixir outside and poured it on the crushed gods, making a commitment to never need either of them again. Then Apphia put the gold in a safe place. They quickly headed for the bedroom to try and get at least a few minutes of sleep before work began.

In the early morning light, Beryl glanced across the room as Apphia was getting ready for bed. Pure beauty and flowing gracefulness, Apphia glowed with life. Noticing Beryl's eye-catching glance Apphia was mesmerized, bold strength combined with passion, a striking man of great resolve. Beryl moved close giving Apphia a tender hug. They kissed and quietly slipped into the bed. Acutely intense, deeply relaxing, time passed unnoticed. Peaceful tenderness, great strength, life flowed and the earth moved. ☞

Chapter 15

Jag's Secret Revealed

꒰

Having laid off shore in the harbor for three days with only small parties coming and going from the ship in the skiff, Jag received orders that he could take leave of the Twin Brothers at first light but must return in twenty four hours as they needed to dock the vessel and unload their cargo as soon as the winds would allow it. Sailing under Captain Gracchus proved challenging as his inexperience constantly reminded Jag how fortunate he had been to sail under Capt. Warnken's wise direction. Jag had no doubt that Capt. Warnken could have docked

Shanesse the same day they arrived here in Malta, as the winds were favorable but a bit brisker than Captain Gracchus was currently comfortable with. He was now overly cautious after the costly docking mishap back in Ostia. Jag quietly did his work and made it a point not to complain, although he was very pleased that this trip was only to Malta and back. Jag was far more familiar with traveling to and from the distant points of the civilized world, sometimes a whole year went by before he returned to Ostia. Shanesse would depart with payroll in gold and silver coins and returned with tax monies and rare treasures from the far reaches of the Empire. But he signed on with Captain Gracchus for this short trip carrying general provisions and trade items to Malta and back because he had to return to Ostia for the court trial that was scheduled for the captain and crew of Shanesse in reference to the shipwreck and the great financial loss that was incurred.

Setting foot on Malta strangely felt like home as Jag stepped out of the skiff onto the low dingy docks and climbed the ladder up to the main docks. Hailing a coach, Jag made his way straight to Publius' estate, anxious to see how his friends were doing. It had only been a few months but he really missed his new acquaintances. The love he felt for others, especially those who served the One True God was not something he was accustomed to. He had protected himself in the past by carefully staying disconnected with those he met while shore side, knowing that when he set sail, he may well never see them again. Some of the sailors had women in every port and spent their entire wages on hollow empty relationships that regularly ended up with broken hearted sailors who in turn would search for new women in a new city to trust and to love. To their dismay, their efforts to mend their broken hearts with a new relationship only further destroyed them and the cycle continued.

"The countryside looks so lush and green," Jag commented to the coach driver.

The driver replied, "Things haven't been the same around here since Paul spent the winter."

Surprised, Jag commented, "Paul?"

"Everyone knows Paul," he said. "Since you arrived as crew aboard the Twin Brothers, I knew you would know Paul."

Almost embarrassed about being associated with the Twin Brothers, Jag quickly replied, "This is my first trip as crew aboard Twin Brothers."

"Oh," the driver quickly replied, "Paul was aboard Shanesse, a ship that wrecked off shore here last winter, and he healed everyone that was sick on the entire island." Excitedly the driver continued, not giving Jag a moment to speak, "Everyone knows Paul. Paul sailed for Rome aboard your ship early this spring; that's why I was sure you would know him. That sure was a terrible storm," he randomly continued, not slowing for a second. "I've never seen a Nor'easter like that one before, but it was ultimately to our benefit. Paul saved the entire shipload of people!"

Catching his breath, the driver stopped just for an instant and Jag quickly interjected, "I too was aboard Shanesse. Paul is a personal friend of mine."

Swinging around in his seat to see Jag, the driver reached out his hand and excitedly said, "Wendell, my name is Wendell." Vigorously shaking Jag's hand he continued, "You're a friend of Paul! It sure is nice to meet you. What did you say your name was?" he asked. But allowing no time for Jag to respond Wendell rattled on. "How's Paul doing? I'm sure they set him free by now; there's no reason to hold that man prisoner. He's a true man of God. This island will never be the same since he was here. You see how green everything is. The fruits and vegetables are growing bigger, and there's more of them than ever before. It's all because of the One True God that Paul spoke of." Barely taking time for another breath, Wendell excitedly continued his unpredictable dialogue. "Paul taught us many things of God while he was here. We would go out to Publius' estate every afternoon to hear his words, but I guess you already know that, you would have been there also. But what you may not know is that our local fishermen are catching bigger fish and more of them than ever before. This island will never be the same," he said as they pulled up to the front door of Publius' mansion.

Climbing out of the coach, Jag paid Wendell and thanked him for the ride.

"It sure was nice talking with you," Wendell said as he urged his horses ahead. "A friend of Paul, that's incredible. I just met a personal friend of Paul," Jag heard him saying as he drove away.

Jag had every intention of correcting his mistaken statement of this being his first trip as crew aboard the Twin Brothers, having remembered that he was employed on the trip from Malta to Rome also but it had become clear that there was no time for explanation, in fact there was no time for anything but listening when a body found himself riding in Wendell's coach.

Standing there laughing and shaking his head, Jag was greeted by one of the servants and invited in.

Publius met him in the entranceway and said, "Just in time for breakfast my friend, will you join us?" Looking more closely he said, "Jag? Is that you, Jag! How are you doing? It's so good to see you again. This truly is an unexpected surprise."

"It's me," Jag said shaking Publius' hand.

"Have you come aboard the Twin Brothers?"

"Yes," Jag said, "I'm sailing again."

"I saw it was laying in the harbor waiting for favorable winds for a few days." "Please, won't you join us for breakfast?" Publius asked, ushering Jag into the dining hall. "Look who's here," Publius said loudly, "This is Jag, one of the sailors that was with Paul and Luke, in case any of you haven't met him." Showing him to one of the couches, Publius took the one next to him. Slipping off his sandals, one of the servants came and washed Jag's feet. Publius offered a prayer of thanksgiving and breakfast began.

"Has Paul been set free?" Publius asked.

"No," Jag said, "He's still awaiting his trial, as are we. The trial for the loss of Shanesse hasn't even taken place yet. I have to be back in Ostia within two months for that."

"Sorry to hear that," Publius said, "I'm sure you'll be acquitted for the loss of Shanesse. No one could possibly prove negligence. I sent official papers along with Capt. Warnken documenting the worst Nor'easter we've ever experienced."

Others were chatting at the table about the tremendous abundance that was being experienced on Malta.

"Have you noticed how beautiful the island looks?" Publius asked.

"I have," Jag replied and then laughing he continued, "I also got a high speed overview of the incredible blessings you have been enjoying on my ride here."

Everyone laughed and three of them said in unison, "You met Wendell."

Still laughing and nodding his head Jag said, "He's a great guy."

"He really is," Publius said, "But it's impossible to hold a conversation with him. He gets so excited and talks so fast, that you must just hold on to your seat and go for the ride."

The staff worked quietly and proficiently. No one really noticed the breakfast was cleared with the exception of some dried fruit and a few small bowls of nuts. Publius and the others told Jag of the local economy that had experienced nothing less than a miraculous increase and of many who continued to teach what they learned from Paul, Luke and Aristarchus. Various meetings were held daily around the island, encouraging the people to remain loyal to the One True God and live according to His Kingdom principles and standards. Jag said how disappointed he was to bring the sad news of how many people that had survived the shipwreck had seemingly forgotten the three months of teaching here on the island. The pressure of their schedules and the loss of their goods became a reality for them back on the mainland and the things of God seemed to slip into the background.

Getting up from the table, it was nearly time for the noon meal as Publius took Jag to an inner room in the mansion and showed him a vast amount of wealth in gold and silver and precious stones.

"Could you personally oversee the shipment of this, back to Rome?" Publius asked, pointing to the sorted and counted money and precious stones.

"What is all this?" Jag asked.

"We so appreciate Paul, Luke and Aristarchus having brought the good news of the Kingdom to us here on Malta that we set aside ten percent of our increase. This too is a principal of the Kingdom of the One True God and we are honored to help them as they have helped us."

Jag explained that the best way to ship the money was to pack it tightly in small wooden boxes so it would not jingle when handled and label the boxes "tools". In this way, it would attract no undue attention and could be safely shipped.

Publius needed to preside over an official meeting so he took his leave of Jag and disappeared into the small elegant hall reserved for such occasions. Jag walked into the gorgeous garden and sat on one of the benches enjoying the afternoon. Hearing beautiful singing, Jag turned to see a lovely young lady strolling through the tall bushes in the garden. Noticing Jag, she walked over to his bench and asked if she could join him. Amazed and impressed with her boldness, he slid to the side and she sat down.

"I enjoyed your singing," he said trying to start a conversation.

"I was singing praises to my Lord, His name is Jesus. Do you know Him?"

Completely astonished at the boldness of this young gorgeous woman, Jag simply replied, "Yes, He's my Lord also."

"My name is Jasmine," she said without any hesitation, "What's your name?"

"Jag," he said feeling just a bit uncomfortable as she looked directly into his eyes, completely self-assured and unabashed.

"Jag," she said smiling, that's surely not your real name, that's just what people call you, right?"

Without even thinking he told her something that few people other than his own family back in Alexandria knew, "My name is Javolenus."

"That's a fine name," Jasmine said, "but I'll just call you Jag, is that ok?"

"That would be just all right," he said with a big smile. Really beginning to like this young lady Jag asked, "Do you live here on the island or are you here with one of the dignitaries?"

"I live here on the island with one of the dignitaries," Jasmine said. "My father is Publius."

Taken aback Jag's mouth nearly dropped open as he exclaimed with surprise, "Publius?"

"Yes," she said, "I believe you must have met him as this is his garden that you're relaxing in."

"Yes, yes, I know him," Jag kind of blurted out, "But where were you this last winter? I would surely have noticed someone as beautiful as you."

"I was in Rome in school," she replied.

"In school?" Jag asked again with a look of great surprise. "But you're a girl," he said.

"Oh," she said laughing, "I'm glad you noticed."

They talked for hours, both gaining much respect for the other. Jag was highly educated himself having grown up in Alexandria, the intellectual capital of the world and also came from a very well to do family. But he had never met a lady like Jasmine. It was immensely refreshing for him to talk with such a bold, knowledgeable, young lady who loved the Lord as much as he did.

Jag had gone to sea to find himself, much to his family's dismay. He had all the schooling, money and influence a man could desire but something was missing. He told no one about his family, not even his best friends. He wanted to prove himself as just an ordinary sailor and in the last five years he excelled at that. Then he finally found the fulfillment that he was looking for sitting under Paul's teaching last winter.

Having nearly completed his twenty four hours of leave, it was early in the morning and Jag was riding back to the docks in one of Publius' carriages. He had made arrangements with Publius to return for the shipment he had requested Jag oversee as soon as they began to reload the ship, but first it must be offloaded. As the carriage approached the docks, Jag was surprised to see the Twin Brothers tied up there. They had brought it in yesterday during his leave, he wondered how the docking went this time. He didn't have to wonder long as he saw a long gouge stretching most of the way along it's hull and damage to the docks that were being repaired as the cargo was being offloaded. Asking the carriage driver to wait, Jag went aboard the Twin Brothers, collected his wages and terminated his employment with that unskilled group of amateurs. Returning to the estate, he was again just in time for breakfast. At the breakfast table he explained to Publius that he would be transporting his shipment to Paul via another ship and explained his disgust with the Twin Brothers.

At Publius' invitation, Jag remained on the island for another six weeks. During this time he located another vessel bound for Ostia who carried the Gold Seal of Caesar. He was a great deal more comfortable carrying the precious gift of Malta back to Paul on a certified vessel with an experienced Captain and a proper crew.

Publius requested that Jag accompany him to more than one official meeting with foreign dignitaries, and their friendship grew as Jag showed exceptional abilities and insights in this area.

But every free moment was filled with Jasmine. If Jag was not with her, he was thinking about her. For the first time in many years, he considered revealing his secret. He had guarded his heart so well during all his years at sea. And his past, no one knew his secret, not even his close friends Nassor, Mecho and Ulray especially. To them he was a top quality sailor who without hesitation would place his life on the line for ship and crew. He was also an exceptional friend who they could trust, but for some unknown reason he never spoke of his past, even if questioned. His friends accepted that and life went on.

But Jasmine, within five minutes of meeting her she had extracted his real name, something no one else had accomplished since he had gone to sea. Their friendship grew and where one was found, the other was sure to be there also. Now the question arose, should he divulge his secret identity to Jasmine? Maybe later he thought; as of now he wanted to know if she was interested in him, not just his family and the great wealth and status that they represented.

One evening, Jag received word that Publius would like to speak with him alone. Curious, Jag welcomed the opportunity to visit and made his way to the meeting place. Publius smiled at Jag and said, "I got to know you quite well over the three months you lived here with me and have a tremendous respect for you as you handle yourself well. You were quiet but there was something about you that I couldn't figure out back then. You always sat in on Paul's meetings with the dignitaries and you quietly fit in, asking interesting questions and discussing very unlikely things with them. I wondered a few times, how does a sailor fit so comfortably with these men? Then I saw you diligently weigh out this teaching of Paul and after careful consideration you accepted his words and solidly took a stand for the King and His Kingdom. I remember thinking as you left with the others, what an extraordinary sailor!

"Last night Jasmine came to me, completely enthralled with this man she met only a few weeks ago. Jasmine is twenty years old, well educated and confident. She severely intimidates men twice her age, not purposefully but she knows who she is and can see, without difficulty, straight through men who want a female puppet to do their bidding. But last night she came to me and asked if I'd consider arranging a marriage for her with a sailor. I knew for some time already that she had fallen for you. I normally wouldn't consider arranging a marriage for my daughter with a sailor, she deserves more, but with you, I liked you from the start. Then she goes on to say that your name is Javolenus.

"Javolenus my friend, I know your father don't I? He spoke of Javolenus, the son who was very discontent and had to 'find himself'. You look just like your father, Jag. I can not believe I didn't recognize you sooner. Your family rules Alexandria, how did you end up as a sailor aboard Shanesse?"

"This is all true my friend," Jag said. "My father did visit here multiple times but before we speak any further of arranging a marriage, I must let you know that Jasmine stole something of mine."

Greatly surprised at this accusation Publius, with a very serious look on his face asked, "What?"

"It happened shortly after I arrived. I didn't miss it until I got to the docks and, boarded Twin Brothers six weeks ago. I cleaned out my quarters and it wasn't there. Looking at Jasmine who just walked into the room and had no idea what was being discussed, Jag pointed at her and said, "She stole my heart, and if you look closely you will see she has it in her possession."

Smiling hugely Publius agreed, "Yes, she has it! She's had it for quite awhile now I have noticed. She personally has come to me and requested that I arrange a marriage for her with the one whose heart she holds so gently in her hands."

Jag replied, in a most commanding tone of voice, as if he was presiding over a very important diplomatic meeting, "I see no alternative than to agree to a marriage as soon as possible."

Jasmine's face told it all, with a huge smile she walked over to Jag holding out her cupped hands, "Do you want it back?" she asked.

"Jasmine, you are an extraordinary lady," Jag said, tenderly embracing her and kissing her cheek. There is something I must tell you." He went on to explain his secret in depth and assure her that there would be no more secrets between them. ☞

Chapter 16

Nassor Steps In

This early in the day? Nassor wondered, "the sun is still below the horizon and there's already people here doing business? A horse and cart waited outside and the door stood partially open with muffled voices coming from inside. Walking into the dimly lit room, something did not feel right. The hair on the back of his neck stood on end as a shadowy figure in the far corner seemed to be struggling to get up. If it was not so early in the morning Nassor would have guessed the man was very intoxicated, but as his eyes adjusted to the dimly lit room, he noticed three aggressive looking characters standing around someone else on the floor in the other corner. Nassor instinctively scanned the situation as his mind raced back to the days of defending Shanesse from bands of raiders. A bench nearby stood in the early morning light that was streaming through the partially open front door. It had a nicely carved table leg laying on it that looked much like the columns that were used so prevalently in this area for building. With a small rounded base, a slender cylinder shape with a capital on top and square stock protruding above the capital for attaching it to a table, it was not just a table leg, but a finely finished piece of artwork. Having small intricate clusters of grapes carved into the top, hanging down over the capital, it was one of those well done pieces that caught Nassor's eye even in the dim morning light. Walking over to the bench, admiring the table leg Nassor picked it up and looked at it more closely as he keenly watched the activity in the far corner of the room.

Nassor spoke in a strong confident voice, "Good morning gentlemen."

One of the tough looking fellows in the corner growled, "We're not open, come back later."

Nassor laid the table leg back on the bench and boldly pressed on, "I need to visit with the master."

Two of the three spun around and faced him, hiding the man on the floor from view as best as they could. The man on the right produced a knife and the one on the left had arms as big around as an average fellow's legs. The men were poorly shaved with straggly hair and bad attitudes. Acting as if he had not recognized anything out of the ordinary, Nassor turned his back on the activity in the corner and faced the bench again.

The huge one growled, "I told you we aren't open. You'll have to come back later."

Nassor leaned on the bench strategically placing his right hand on the narrow end of the table leg and said, "I traveled a great distance, I guess I'll have to wait."

The huge man walked heavily over to the door and kicked it wide open bellowing, "Get out now!"

Nassor did not respond. Out of the corner of his eye Nassor saw the man as large as a bear standing in the doorway motioning for him to leave the building. Then with strong profanities the huge giant of a man rushed towards Nassor as the other two ruffians eagerly watched from their corner, expecting their powerful accomplice to literally toss this ignorant intruder out the front door.

With one smooth motion Nassor stepped aside and the table leg in his right hand swept around with the speed of a piece of debris in a Nor'easter, connecting with the man's chest which was round as a barrel. A deep forceful oomph was heard along with multiple ribs fracturing as his large form collapsed over the bench where Nassor had been standing.

The other two reacted resourcefully, separating and simultaneously coming at Nassor from both sides, one with his knife and the other had a short sword that had been kept well concealed until now. The evil character with the sword was not swinging it viciously about but held it steady in a thrusting position. These were no ordinary commoners who found themselves with random weapons and had wrongly chosen to seize the opportunity to increase their spending money. Nassor suddenly realized these were hardened raiders, experienced killers. Dropping to the floor Nassor threw the table leg with blinding speed, carrying no spin it flew blunt end first with pinpoint accuracy and connected with his assailant's left knee. Hearing a distinct snap as tendons ruptured from the tremendous impact, the sword fell to the floor as the man clutched his knee that had buckled unnaturally to the side. Rolling out of the way as the very angry third attacker descended upon him, Nassor grabbed the man's wrist as this thug handled his knife in a very deadly fashion. This killer did not hold the knife high in the air with the blade facing down as most inexperienced assailants would, he held the blade close and facing up with every intention of bringing it up under the rib cage and piercing the heart. Now acutely aware that these men were experienced murderers a deep resolve rose up in Nassor much the same as when he fought for Shanesse; lives may be lost today but his would not be one of them. With the extreme strength of one who grips lines and sets sails for a living, Nassor slowly forced the knife in his assailant's hand right up under the man's chin. Terror flooded the man's face as he gradually gave way to the powerful sailor's grip.

Nassor said through gritted teeth, "If I hadn't met Jesus a few months ago you would surely meet Him today," and with a fierce twist of his powerful wrist, the man's forearm snapped and the knife fell to the floor.

"Don't even move," Nassor said forcefully as he picked up the weapons and stuck the sword in his belt. Walking over to the man on the floor in the corner, Nassor recognized Beryl, the man who he saw at the dinner table at Paul's house. Kneeling down and helping him up Nassor asked, "Are you ok my friend?"

A little shaken from being knocked down repeatedly Beryl said, "I think so," as he got up.

Turning to the two assailants laying on the floor, one holding his arm tightly and the other still rolling around on the floor holding his knee Nassor said, "Get out now," then shouting in a deep commanding voice he said, pointing to the huge hulk of a man that was now doubled up on the floor by the bench trying to breath, "And take that big piece of trash

with you!" Making his way over to the other man
who was trying to get up when he entered the room,
he bent down to help him gently to his feet and over
to a couch by the wall. Helping him lay down
Nassor noticed a huge bump on his head, spinning
around Nassor shouted, "You urchins are going to
prison and you should be very pleased about that!
Normally I'd simply rid the earth of reprobates like
you! You beat this man and tried to kill me!"

Learning from Beryl that the morning watch
would be through town in fifteen or twenty minutes
Nassor followed the three men as they struggled
helping each other out the door and into their
wagon. Then he tied the men's hands and feet then
lashed them to the floor of their own wagon.

Demanding that they not be turned over to the
authorities lest they return and finish the job at a
later date, Nassor realized that even in defeat they
showed no remorse. As the authorities arrived they
immediately recognized the three men, as the only
survivors from a notorious band of rebels that had
been annihilated by Roman soldiers in a skirmish
earlier that month. Rarely was a rebel group found
this close to Rome as the countryside was normally
quiet and peaceful with a strong presence of Roman
rule securely established.

Apphia came over to the shop to let Beryl and
their slave know that breakfast was ready just as the
authorities were leaving with the three hoodlums

and their wagon. The remainder of their staff was arriving for work and Beryl of course insisted that Nassor join them for breakfast. Beryl was a bit bruised up but very talkative as he explained the entire morning's events in great detail to his very grateful Apphia who had many questions of her own. Their slave who had been struck on the head was feeling much better although he did not want breakfast and was quite content to have the day off.

Beryl said, "It's sure a good thing that we keep the gold in the house and not over in our shop where they were looking for it."

Apphia replied, "Beryl, you should have given it to them, they may have killed you."

"Yes but those evil men probably would have killed us even after we gave them the gold. It's very fortunate that Nassor happened along at the perfect time." Turning to Nassor he asked, "What were you doing out and about that early in the morning anyway?"

Nassor smiled and said, "I left Rome last night, I enjoy traveling at night; it reminds me of life at sea."

Breakfast was nearly over when Apphia asked, "Nassor, did Beryl get your furniture order together for you?"

"I didn't come for furniture."

With a puzzled look of amazement Beryl asked, "Why did you come?"

"I have been staying with Paul in Rome," Nassor said.

Very surprised Beryl quickly said, "We're not finished with his order yet, that was only three weeks ago."

"Don't worry," Nassor said, "He was concerned about you, not his furniture order."

Apphia quickly interjected, "I knew God had something to do with this."

Beryl quietly asked, "Paul, the man of God sent you? How does he know all these things? When I arrived at his home, the very first time I met him, he told me the secrets of my heart. Now he sends help that arrives the exact moment that three men try to rob me. We have never been robbed before; in fact we've never really considered the possibility of being robbed."

"You have become a very wealthy man," Nassor said. "You may want to take a few additional precautions as your business continues to prosper."

"Yes," Beryl replied, "I suppose you're right. I haven't thought much about that."

Nassor continued, "I don't know if Paul knew about the attempted robbery this morning or not, but you can be certain that the God who we both serve knew about it."

Surprised again Beryl questioned, "You have accepted Jesus as Lord?"

"That I have my friend, that I have," Nassor replied. "Fortunately for those three men this morning because in years gone by, I'd have ended their lives right then and there."

Apphia asked quietly, "Were you a murderer before you met Jesus?"

"No," Nassor said, "My job was to protect other people's valuables that were being shipped aboard our vessel, which sometimes put me face to face with those who would kill for personal gain. You must understand that most times I've faced men of that sort, there's no morning watch or any other kind of law enforcement anywhere near."

"So you would just kill them?" Apphia asked.

"You do realize," Nassor replied, "That the Roman soldiers recognized them as outlaws the moment they saw them, and they are sure to die even without a court trial by noon today unless by some outside chance those ruffians are citizens of Rome, which I doubt."

"Please don't misunderstand me," Apphia said, "I am extremely grateful that you saved Beryl's life. What I have difficulty understanding is how we're supposed to love people. Luke told Beryl that we're supposed to lay ourselves and our interests aside and make it work for others."

"Jesus is our example," Nassor said.

"Yes, that's what Luke told Beryl also, Jesus is our example," Apphia agreed.

"Ok," Nassor said, "And our friend Luke also speaks of a time when Jesus sent out his disciples and told them to take no staff, no bread and no money and they went. Another time Jesus instructs his disciples that they should take their money bag, a knapsack and if they didn't have a sword, they should buy one. With these two examples seeming to be completely opposite, I believe we must hear clearly what to do in each situation, not just try to do the same thing every time.

"As I walked into the display room this morning, I saw three ruffians threatening the lives of Beryl and his slave. To love someone is to lay your life down for that person; in this case I had three choices. If I loved my life I had the opportunity to walk out and not get involved. If I loved the life of crime, I could have helped them retrieve the gold and quickly become rich. But if I loved the shop owner and defended his ways of doing an honest business, I had to place myself in harm's way and defend what I believed was the godly choice.

"So you see my love for Beryl and protecting him and his business may not look like love at all if you were one of the three thugs that had to be disabled so they didn't murder someone this morning. I have no love for the lifestyle that those murderers have chosen, and they clearly had no interest in the ways of Jesus, so this afternoon they will receive their just reward and die for their lives of crime.

You see Apphia," Nassor explained, "Laying yourself and your interests aside and inviting the criminals into your home for breakfast and then giving them all your gold is not the love that Jesus spoke of. They would have eaten your food, taken your gold and then killed your husband right before your eyes, then you could turn the other cheek, also words of Jesus, and they would have abused you then killed you as well. Now the question remains, with your children being left as orphans and your gold supporting three murderers, would that have promoted the kingdom of God or the kingdom of the enemy? Acts of love that Jesus spoke about will always promote the kingdom of the One True God but will look differently in different situations. We must listen to the voice of the Holy Spirit in every situation to know the way of Love."

With further explanation, both Beryl and Apphia asked for and received the Holy Spirit as Nassor laid hands on them and prayed.

Nassor accompanied Beryl to the shop where he showed him the different tools of the trade and how they made furniture. Very interested in the intricate carving on some of the finer pieces of furniture, Beryl gave Nassor a lesson in carving and how to choose the proper wood grain patterns to give the project a distinctive style of its own.

Beryl invited Nassor to stay with his family and teach them more about the One True God and His Kingdom for a few days and Nassor agreed. The days stretched into weeks and the weeks to months as Nassor taught Beryl and his family the things that he had learned sitting under the teaching of Paul, Luke and Aristarchus for ninety days on Malta and nearly ninety days since that in the city of Rome.

Nassor was a talented teacher, and Beryl had been telling everyone about his Jesus. Soon the display room of Beryl's shop was filled to capacity each evening as Nassor would train the many locals that accepted Beryl's Jesus in the ways of His Kingdom. Beryl's two younger daughters Francis who was twelve and very pleased to be turning thirteen later this year and Lusius his eight year old both accepted Jesus and were notably more stress-free and pleasant as they went about their duties each day. Odilia was still very disappointed with her father for exposing her little sister and refused to look at him when she visited her mother.

Odilia had fallen ill and could not get out of her bed for over a week when Beryl took the morning off and traveled across town to see her. Entering her bedroom he was appalled to see just how weak she was as she struggled to look away when she saw her daddy come through the door. Beryl sat quietly by her bed and explained as best he could why he had exposed his little girl, how he could not see any other options at the time. He told her of the terrible dreams he had hearing his little girl crying 'Recognize me, daddy. Please recognize me'. Odilia began weakly crying as she tried to ignore her father's words. Then he told Odilia that his mental anguish at night made him seek help to sleep and about being addicted to the elixir of sleep and how it poisoned his body. Then Beryl went on to explain how he had found forgiveness and new life in Jesus and how Jesus healed his shaky body over the following weeks.

Then quietly Beryl asked, "Odilia, will you please forgive me? I was wrong, and I lost two daughters that day. Will you please forgive me?" Laying his hands on his precious Odilia he prayed, "Father, my Lord and my God, please show Odilia you love her. Be made whole in Jesus Name!" he commanded.

At that instant his hands felt like they were on fire and Odilia leaped from her bed. Completely astounded, Beryl's mouth dropped open as he also jumped to his feet. Odilia hugged him tightly sobbing and quivering as she said, "I forgive you Daddy, I forgive you."

Beryl had believed the stories of Paul and others praying for people and them instantly getting healed, but he was literally astounded that his Lord had instantly healed Odilia at his request. Her color had returned and she looked well.

Wide-eyed Odilia explained, "It felt like you poured burning oil on my shoulders and it surged through my whole being. I couldn't stay in bed, I was on fire. I thought if I die right now, the last thing I want to do is forgive you, but I'm well; I feel great! Jesus healed me! I want Jesus as my Lord."

Odilia heard much of Beryl's Jesus through Apphia the last few weeks but now she kneeled down with her daddy and prayed right there in the room. Beryl also whispered a prayer of his own, "Lord it is so good to have my daughter back. Thank you for healing her, and Odilia accepting you, I couldn't ask for more. Thank You, Thank You, Lord. I love you."

That evening Odilia and her husband joined the crowd of people gathered at Beryl's furniture shop to hear Nassor speak. Francis snuggled up to her big sister and listened intently to Nassor's account of being shipwrecked with Paul and how the One True God had saved them all from the sea.

"Isn't he awesome?" Francis asked Odilia.

"Sure is," Odilia agreed, "He healed me this morning and Daddy and I are actually talking again."

"Yeah I know," Francis said, "But Nassor, isn't he awesome too? You know he saved Daddy's life? Professional killers with knives and swords and Nassor took three of them down at the same time with nothing more than a table leg."

Odilia looked over at Francis and smiled, all of a sudden realizing that her little sister was growing up. Francis was starry eyed and plainly smitten by this new friend of Daddy's.

"I'd love to go to sea sometime, wouldn't you Odilia?" Francis asked.

"Yes," Odilia said, "I believe that would be nice, but I think you would enjoy it a lot more than I would."

"What do you mean, I would like it better?"

Odilia laughed, "Nassor would be there," she said.

"Oh stop it," Francis said, "I just think it would be nice to go to sea."

"Yes, I know, I know," Odilia said and winked at Francis.

Elbowing her big sister, Francis blushed and smiled awkwardly.

Nassor spent many hours building a truly amazing scale model of Shanesse. It had tremendous detail and was a valuable work of art when he completed it nearly a month later. Nassor had inlaid a gold coin into the base that he had built to support his model ship. The coin had Caesar's head on the one side but it had the prow of Shanesse on the reverse side. Coins of this type were prevalent throughout the Empire of Rome, and Nassor was quite pleased to have Shanesse on a gold aureus as the Twin Brothers was on a silver denarius. The gold aureus was worth twenty five silver denarii. At about the same time he completed the model, Nassor received a message from Paul.

The letter read: "There is a fine vessel laying in the Ostia harbor whose owner is looking for a captain. The previous captain fell ill and the owner tried desperately to hire Capt. Warnken because of his excellent reputation. However he turned the job down and recommended you for the position, Nassor. You need to report to the docks in two weeks. Please stop by my house on your way. I have something for you. Signed, Your Friend, Paul."

Very excited about the opportunity, Nassor informed Beryl that he would teach the evening meetings for one more week but then Beryl would have to take over as he was going back to sea. Nassor took Beryl into town to a small eatery for lunch and as they were chatting about everything from ministry to sailing he stopped. Looking his friend in the eye he asked, "Beryl, I know it's not your custom for things to be handled like this, but I have a very important favor to ask of you."

Beryl quickly replied, "Nassor, my friend, I'll help you in any way I can. I recognize you as a great man of God and not only that, I owe you my life."

Nassor smiled and looked around the room a bit.

"What is it my friend?" Beryl asked. "What is your request?"

Nassor looked back at Beryl who now was leaning forward as to try and withdraw the request from his new best friend. Nassor said, "Beryl, I would like to ask," and he stopped again, searching for words, no, searching for courage.

"What can be this important, my friend?" Beryl asked. "I've never seen you without words Nassor."

Nassor smiled and looked down at the table. Looking back at Beryl he said, "I'd like to ask you for Francis' hand in marriage." "Not now," he quickly added, "I know you prefer that your girls be fifteen, and I'm willing to wait two years for Francis if it's ok with you. I'm twenty seven now so I'll be twenty nine in two years."

"That, my friend is a very easy question," Beryl said with a smile. "I know of no one that I'd rather she marry. I am much more interested in a man of quality than a man of exactly twenty five years of age. You my friend are a man of quality. You know she loves you Nassor. Or didn't you notice how she shadows you in the shop every minute she's not busy with her own work. I hear her talking to her mother of how great it would be to go to sea."

"I too have feelings for her," Nassor said, "She's so pleasant, always full of energy. She has her mother's beauty and her father's great resolve. I would be deeply honored if you would arrange for our marriage in two years. We may not be able to visit very often if I'm working as captain," Nassor explained. "But I'll treat her with respect and honor as a child of our King, not just as a wife."

Standing up and shaking Nassor's hand Beryl said, "Consider it done my friend, Francis will be very happy."

"Your acceptance has made me very happy," Nassor said as they walked out of the eatery.

It seemed as if only moments had passed but the week was gone and Nassor was saying his goodbyes. The little ones gave him big hugs and Apphia also gave him a hug. Beryl walked over and gave Nassor a huge hug and whispered in his ear. "She doesn't know, you tell her," and nodded toward the corner where Francis was quietly standing.

Nassor looked at Francis and asked, "Well, are you going to give me a hug, too?"

With the personal invitation, Francis timidly walked over and hugged him tightly, not wanting to ever let him go. As she released her grip and turned to walk away, Nassor held her at arm's length and looked into her beautiful blue eyes.

A tear flowed down her cheek as she whispered, "I wish you didn't have to leave."

Squeezing her shoulders tightly Nassor said, "I'll be back for you, in two years we will be married, your father is making the arrangements."

Her eyes widened in delight with the most beautiful sparkle that Nassor had ever seen. Looking toward her father, Nassor smiled and released his grip on her shoulders. Glancing at her daddy she saw him nod his approval and she simply launched into Nassor's arms nearly knocking him over, giving him the biggest hug, burying her face in his shirt and shedding tears of pure joy. Regaining her composure and thinking she must act like a young lady, Francis took a deep breath, wiped her eyes, stood up tall and simply beamed with a smile of deep satisfaction. Second only to Jesus being her Lord, this was the best news she'd ever heard. She was so pleased.

As a memento, Nassor gave Francis his masterpiece, the model of Shanesse that he had so meticulously constructed. It was in fact one of the very few things he owned since his stay on Malta. Shanesse stood prominently on an elaborately carved base with the inlaid coin elegantly displaying her prow in gold. Promising his return, he climbed aboard his wagon and set a course for Rome. ☛

Chapter 17

Pharos of the Sea

Arriving in front of Paul's house, Mecho met Nassor in the driveway. "Captain Nassor," he thundered, "Are you in need of an able bodied seaman?"

"No sir," Nassor barked, "My crew positions are all full up. I have need of a first class officer, strong and powerful in word and deed, one who knows the ropes and can brilliantly lead, one who will be second only to the captain."

Jumping off the wagon, the two men grabbed each other in a rough sailor style hug and laughed heartily.

Walking into Paul's house Nassor said, "Seriously my friend, it would be a great honor to have you as second in command. Someone who I know and can count on, I thought of you the moment I received the letter. It'll be great to sail the seas again. Have you heard anything about the vessel?"

Mecho said, "Nothing other than Capt. Warnken highly recommending you as captain and we both know he wouldn't consider an inferior ship."

"I thought the same thing," Nassor said. "If Capt. Warnken recommends the position, she's a fine vessel."

Nassor gave Paul a gift from Beryl, that included a letter assuring him that their group was praying for him and his ministry team every day and thanking him for sending Nassor who not only saved his life the day he arrived but stayed and taught the good news of the Kingdom every day since. Included was a substantial financial gift that represented ten percent of the profits from the furniture business over the last few months. Paul in turn gave both Nassor and Mecho a sizeable financial gift in return for their services.

Taking leave of Paul, Nassor and Mecho traveled to the Tiber River accompanied by Luke and Aristarchus. With many well wishes and multiple good-byes Luke and Aristarchus saw their friends off and returned to Paul. Nassor and Mecho boarded a barge for the fifteen and one half mile float down the Tiber River to Ostia. Arriving in town, they secured rooms at the inn by the Basilica where they would have to stand trial in three days. Walking the docks, they speculated which vessel was in need of a captain. Multiple vessels lined the docks, and they recognized the Twin Brothers laying at anchor a short distance out in the harbor.

Mecho asked, "Suppose Captain Gracchus is waiting for an opening here on the docks or do you think he brought the skiff ashore, looking for Capt. Warnken to dock that thing for him?"

"Actually it's rather frightening to see someone so inexperienced captain a vessel of that size," Nassor said.

Mecho thoughtfully replied, "It really is. There are many lives aboard a vessel of that size. I wonder who Gracchus knew to land a captain's position aboard the Twin Brothers?"

Nassor replied, "You do realize that we have to stand trial in three days because of men like Captain

Gracchus don't you. He could successfully pile the Twin Brothers up on the rocks in a small gale because of gross negligence."

"How much damage is allowed before there's a trial?" Mecho asked.

"It's usually not an issue unless government property like taxes or payroll is lost or if there is loss of life," Nassor replied.

"Like when we arrived and Captain Gracchus tried to sail right up town and dock by the Thermopolium so Castor and Pollux could get dinner," Mecho asked laughing. "Do you think that mishap could end up in court?"

"Not likely," Nassor said, "That simply involves an embarrassed owner of the Twin Brothers paying damages to, and receiving insults from, the dock master, in reference to his incompetent captain."

A very familiar booming voice called out, "Nassor, do you like her?" Spinning around Nassor recognized Capt. Warnken coming out of the building by the dock. He was pointing down to the end of the docks to a large new vessel that Nassor could not identify.

Catching up to them, Capt. Warnken warmly greeted Nassor and Mecho.

"How are you doing, Captain?" Nassor asked.

"I've been sailing through an endless sea of paperwork," he said shaking his head. "It's been a long voyage but the trial in three days should be nothing more than an official acquittal, as everything has finally been established. The documents from Publius have proven to be the key. He's a highly respected official carrying much authority in the shipping world." Again pointing down the docks, Capt. Warnken asked, "Have you seen Pharos of the Sea?"

"No sir," Nassor replied, "I'm not familiar with her."

Walking down the docks to see the vessel, Mecho spoke up, "Do you know Pharos is the largest lighthouse in the world?"

"Hey," Nassor reminded them, "I'm from Alexandria, Pharos was also the first lighthouse. It remains one of the seven wonders of the world for over two hundred and fifty years by now."

"How tall is it?" Mecho asked. "It looks huge when you sail into port."

"It is," Capt. Warnken replied, "Standing at 443 feet, it's the tallest building in the world."

"The light is directed by mirrors," Nassor said. "That's why you can see it so far out at sea. The sun is reflected by day and fire by night."

"I've seen it over twenty two miles out," Capt. Warnken said.

"What an interesting name for a ship, literally it means Light of the Sea," Nassor commented.

"I like that," Mecho agreed.

"It also could be translated, Enlightened Mind, or Guide of the Sea," Nassor explained, getting notably excited about this new vessel he continued. "Pharos is dedicated to the Savior Gods; Ptolemy Soter (lit. savior) and his wife Berenice."

Capt. Warnken said, "Light of the Sea, dedicated to the Savior God. I too like it, this vessel definitely needs a Captain who serves the One True God!"

Walking up to Pharos of the Sea, Capt. Warnken's strong voice boomed, "Permission to come aboard?"

From the upper deck a clear strong voice rang out, "Permission granted." A young deck hand met the trio by the rail. Recognizing Capt. Warnken he said with a pleasant smile, "Welcome aboard Captain, who may I tell the master is with you today?"

Turning to Nassor, Capt. Warnken said, "This is Captain Nassor," and motioning toward Mecho he said, "And that's first officer, Mecho." Walking tall with squared shoulders the young deck hand escorted his guests aft.

At that moment Jag came topside. The deck hand began to say something but stopped quickly as Nassor, openly astonished, shouted, "Jag, it's really great to see you! How are you doing? Eagerly shaking his hand, Nassor continued. "Look who I have with me, Captain and Mecho!"

"Jag," Capt. Warnken smiled, "It really is good to see you. Have you transferred from the Twin Brothers?"

"I have," Jag, the man of few words, agreed.

Mecho gave him a powerful sailor hug and stood back and looked at him saying, "It's really great to see you, Jag. You're dressed mighty fine for a sailor," he noted. "The Twins must have been good to you," Mecho said laughing. "When did you terminate your employment with Captain Gracchus?" Mecho asked with a playful grin. "Did Castor and Pollux complete the voyage unscathed?

Jag started laughing loudly, "You see the Twins laying out in the harbor, don't you?" he said pointing at the vessel anchored out. "I think they're waiting for Capt. Warnken to take the skiff out there and pilot their vessel safely to the docks. We were laying off Malta just like that when I took a twenty four hour leave and went to see our friend Publius, who is doing great by the way."

"I'd love to visit with Publius again," Nassor said.

"Yes, as would I," Capt. Warnken said and Mecho agreed nodding his head.

"Anyway," Jag continued, "When I returned from my twenty four hour leave, the Twin Brothers was docked."

Laughing Nassor asked, "Did Castor and Pollux look like they met the One True God again?"

"The figurehead wasn't all broken up this time but there was a deep scar about seventy feet long on the port side compliments of another miscalculation. I decided, sailing with that crew was taking my life in my own hands so I went aboard, collected my wages and emptied my quarters."

"I can't blame you Jag, that's simply not acceptable," Capt. Warnken agreed. "If that unfortunate vessel happens upon a storm, we'll not see her again," he said.

"So tell me," Nassor said, "What did you do then?"

Smiling real big Jag said, "I returned to Publius estate, married his daughter and paid for a private stateroom on the next ship leaving for Ostia and here I am, prepared to stand trial with Capt. Warnken."

All three men busted out laughing.

"You are a comical fellow!" Nassor said, continuing he joked, "So you got here, had a few days to spare, bought this ship with your wages from the Twins and now your looking for crew, right."

Laughing Jag said, "I guess that's about it."

"Let me tell you something funny," Nassor said. "I came to accept the job as captain of your new vessel and I brought Mecho along as my first officer."

"That's not funny," Jag said. "Second only to Capt. Warnken you would make an excellent captain."

Enjoying himself immensely Nassor kept things going, "So I get the job?" he asked.

"Consider it done," Jag said.

"One more thing," Nassor requested, "Mecho man here, I do want him to be my first officer."

Mecho chimed in, "I'd make a good first officer."

"That you would," Jag said, pointing to Nassor he continued, "If Captain Nassor has chosen you, the job is yours.

Stopping abruptly, Mecho looking toward the stern said quietly, "That is a stunning looking woman, what's she doing aboard?"

"Careful," Jag said, "she's the owner's wife."

"Really?" Mecho asked.

"Really," Jag said.

Glancing her direction Nassor said, "She really is fine-looking."

"Be quiet," Mecho said, "she's coming over here."

Confidently walking right up to the group, she put her arm around Jag and smiled.

Feeling extremely awkward, Capt. Warnken looked out over the sea as if there was something of interest out there. Mecho just looked down at the floor, and Nassor stepped back a step or two, scanning the area to see if the owner was going to catch his wife with her arm around his friend. He did not want Jag getting fired before the first voyage.

Jag broke the silence and confidently announced, "Gentleman, this is Jasmine." Stopping for a moment, thoroughly enjoying the looks on his stunned friends' faces, he then continued, "Publius' daughter."

Wide-eyed in unbelief with their mouths agape, his three friends had no words.

Jasmine laughed and said, "What were you gentlemen talking about?"

Nassor stammered around trying to put a sentence together that made sense, "Jag said, uhum, Jag said-." Stopping for a moment he tried again. "Are you really Publius' daughter?" Trying to figure things out he slowly continued, "We spent three months living at his house, and I never saw you."

Jasmine laughed and said, "I was in Rome, in school."

"But you're," Mecho stopped short and Jasmine finished his sentence.

"A girl," she said. "Funny, that's exactly what Jag said when I told him. Actually I am very privileged to have an extraordinarily influential father. I have had many opportunities while growing up that most girls never have."

Nassor looked Jag straight in the eye and asked, "Did you buy this ship?"

"I didn't have to; it already belongs to my family."

"Who's your family?" Capt. Warnken asked. "I talked with a young man aboard this vessel weeks ago, he was trying very hard to get me as captain but I recommended Nassor. He thought Nassor was a bit young but I told him I had complete confidence in Nassor and that he couldn't find a better captain anywhere."

"That was my brother," Jag said. "I didn't even know this was my father's ship. I came aboard to see this fine vessel and much to my surprise, my brother occupied the owner's stateroom. He was completely enthralled with my story, as seven years ago I left home to go find myself. Careful not to tell anyone that I was Javolenus of the royal family of Alexandria, I did my best sailing with you, my friends. But I found what I was looking for only while sitting under Paul's teaching. My brother left for Paul's house yesterday, and I agreed to care for Pharos of the Sea. I know we were just playing around, but I really would be pleased to have you as captain, Captain Nassor, and I can't imagine anyone better suited for the first officer position than your choice of Mecho. We have the finest vessel available. We will spread the good news of the Kingdom and be the Lighthouse of the Sea, rededicating Pharos of the Sea to the True Savior Gods: Jesus and His Father. I can pay you more than the average wage, Pharos of the Sea already carries the Gold Seal of Caesar and as officers, you will of course receive a percentage of the net proceeds. Do we have an agreement my friends?"

Completely amazed at their good fortune, Nassor and Mecho promptly agreed. Producing the necessary documents, all the signatures were quickly in place and Jag suggested they go to the Thermopolium for lunch. Enjoying a fantastic lunch and chatting with many of the crew from Shanesse that were in town for the trial, Captain Nassor and Javolenus filled the remaining positions aboard Pharos of the Sea that same afternoon.

On the third day the Basilica was filled with captain and crew of Shanesse, government officials from Rome and multiple business owners who had interests in the cargo that had been thrown overboard. The proceedings took a bit of time as the business owners stated their claims for lost cargo and the government representatives presented their financial losses from the taxes that were being transported from the far reaches of the empire back to Rome. Captain Warnken carried the full responsibility for Shanesse since Benjobo was no longer a free man and was not able to attend the trial. After a detailed account of the storm and his crew's heroic efforts to keep Shanesse from breaking up at sea, Capt. Warnken produced written documents concerning the storm from Publius, proof of his vessel's carrying the Gold Seal of Caesar and documents confirming that no lives were lost.

With both sides completing their presentations, the presiding Judge made his decision and said, "We have accrued great loss on this last voyage but Capt. Warnken has served us faithfully for many years. He has meticulously prepared and presented documentation concerning the exact details of this fateful journey, including proof of the extremely violent Nor'easter that ultimately destroyed Shanesse. I am impressed by the fact that every last man of his devoted crew is standing by his side in this trial today. I fully acquit Captain Warnken and his devoted crew of any negligence."

Addressing the crew he said, "In honor of your devoted loyalty and heroic efforts that saved two hundred and seventy six lives, you will each individually be presented with royal documentation confirming your devoted service to the Roman Empire. Captain Warnken, it will be noted that you and your crew went above and beyond the call of duty and since Caesar himself has recently decreed that he personally will insure those who carry his gold seal, your wages will be paid by his representative waiting in the outer court. This court is dismissed."

The crew rented a royal transport for Capt. Warnken and insisted that they themselves carry it. With Captain riding comfortably inside on a plush sedan chair fit for a king, he opened the curtains wide enjoying the company of his devoted friends. Eight sailors at a time took turns on the long poles, laughing and raising the ends up and down telling Capt. Warnken they wanted him to feel as if he was back on the sea. Nassor and Jag took charge of the forward two corners with Ulray and Mecho on the aft corners, giving all hands a turn carrying their captain.

Captain's powerful voice rang out, "Set us a course for the Thermopolium."

"Aye Captain, the Thermopolium it is," Jag shouted back as he and Jasmine took the forward positions on the starboard pole.

Seventy five crew noisily made their way through town carrying their favorite captain. Jasmine fit right in, not in the slightest bit intimidated by the sailors.

Arriving at the eatery, Nassor shouted orders, "Turn to starboard, coming about...Steady, hold steady." Nassor had them continue to hold the transport high and the sailors formed two lines facing each other, standing shoulder to shoulder they linked arms with the person across from them and fashioned steps with each pair reaching lower to the ground, the last two pairs on their knees.

Opening the door Jasmine said, "Welcome to the Thermopolium Captain, will you join us for lunch?"

Enjoying himself superbly, Capt. Warnken walked down the human gang plank and they all followed him into the eatery.

The following morning at Jag's request, Capt. Warnken presided over the re-dedication of Pharos of the Sea to the True Savior Gods, Jesus and His Father. After the dedication, Capt. Warnken made arrangements with Jag for first class accommodations as a paying passenger to Philippi. Jag gave him the finest quarters in the passenger section of the vessel but refused payment of any kind, assuring Capt. Warnken that it was a great honor to have him aboard. With many of the crew from Shanesse, Captain Nassor felt right at home. Pharos of the Sea was undoubtedly one of the finest vessels afloat. Grandly appointed both topside and below, from the majestic carved torch for her figurehead to the stately owner's quarters she excelled in fine craftsmanship. Early afternoon with favorable winds, she sailed out of Ostia harbor on course for Malta.

Jag and Jasmine had successfully delivered the gift from the Maltese Islanders to Paul, watched the mighty hand of the One True God orchestrate a nearly unbelievable progression of events in Ostia; and now with much anticipation, awaited their brief visit to Malta. They carried a letter of encouragement from Paul for the believers on Malta. Then it would be on to Caesarea Philippi to deliver their cargo. ⚑

Chapter 18

Benjobo the Gladiator

The crowd in the amphitheater was aggressive. Benjobo could hear their demands as he awaited his entrance into the arena. Having often attended the games as a wealthy businessman, this was Benjobo's first event as a contestant. The morning had been long as it began with a staged military event where a large number of prisoners of war faced a highly skilled group of soldiers representing the Roman military strength. The ensuing massacre served two causes. First of all, it disposed of a great number of prisoners while depicting the superior strength of the Roman military to the citizens of Rome who were far removed from the battlegrounds. Secondly, it spilled much blood on the sand covering the floor of the amphitheater, which in turn made the following event with savage beasts more exciting. Condemned individuals would face the beasts unarmed and the fresh blood incensed the animals for a ferocious demonstration.

Benjobo was quite young considering the fact that he had come to Rome to retire. But as a wealthy businessman he looked forward to a quieter peaceful life with dreams of finally settling down, getting married and even raising a family. He wanted a stable and caring environment for his children in contrast to the callous hurried world of business that had consumed every waking moment of his adult life. But the stark reality was that he disposed of his savings for retirement with his own hands, somewhere in the middle of a horrible nightmare out in the Mediterranean Sea, in exchange for his life. After which he sat shivering in a cold rain on the shores of Malta, watching his hopes and dreams being dashed to pieces as Shanesse gave way to the forces of the sea.

After much deliberation in his haunting quiet time, Benjobo reasoned there must be more to life! Paul had said, "Give your future to Jesus; He will save you."

But I tried that, he argued with himself silently. I exchanged all my possessions for my life, and I watched others' lives being saved as they rode pieces of my broken dream to shore. What do I get in return? Living on, only to kill in the arena!

Paul brought hope, saved the lives of two hundred and seventy six persons, survived the Naja haje bite, healed all the sick on Malta, and what did he receive? His recompense was coming to Rome as prisoner! Where is his God? Where is justice?

Many prisoners were already annihilated in the games earlier this morning and now more prisoners would face the wild beasts, only to be torn to pieces in front of fifty thousand cheering spectators.

Yes, I made the right decision he assured himself. There is no justice. I shall fight and I shall live! I fought my way up through the ranks of evil twisted men in the business world by my ingenuity and cunning, and I will fight my way up through the ranks of gladiators by my strength and agility. I will do this!

Focus, I must focus, Benjobo thought.

The training had gone exceptionally well, as his lanista was an outstanding teacher. Venting his extreme internal turmoil, Benjobo quickly became a ferocious fighter. Eating specific foods to build strength, training many hours a day and abiding by strict rules of rest time, eating time, meditation time, Benjobo had absolutely no free time. Completely devoted to regaining his honor and buying his freedom, Benjobo looked forward to this day, his first step in proving himself publicly. The sounds of sharpening stones honing weapons to a razor edge could be heard nearby, along with the clatter of various weapons of destruction and armor being fitted on the contestants. There was also the muffled sounds of wild beasts and the crack of whips along with the musical accompaniment depicting the mood of the current contest out in the arena. There was the sickening thud of the heavy mallet hitting the bodies, as the attendant dressed as Pluto, the god of the dead, struck the corpses, to confirm his ownership of the body. The smell of death lingered as another attendant dressed as Mercury, the escorter of souls to the underworld, placed his red hot wand against the fallen victim's flesh to prove the death was authentic.

Benjobo's turn had come. Entering the arena, the sun was bright and the aura of death was heavy. As his eyes adjusted to the light he could see thousands of spectators standing to their feet. This was the contest they really had come to see, highly skilled and trained athletes competing in the games. There were musicians on both sides playing straight trumpets, water organs and large curved instruments called lituus and alongside of them was the couch of Libitina, the Roman goddess of burial, whose next occupant would be the loser of this event.

Benjobo's opponent came out with much fanfare, the crowd clearly recognized this gladiator. His movements were fluid and almost graceful, carrying two swords Benjobo recognized him as a Dimacheri. There are many types of gladiators, and they are paired up according to their lanista's confidence in their abilities. Benjobo, being a Hoplomachi, was more heavily armed than the Dimacheri. Benjobo was wearing leather armor on the shoulders and a mail cuirass protecting his chest, with heavy quilting protecting both legs. Both he and his opponent wore helmets so no one could see their faces. The editor controlled the games but was swayed greatly by the crowd, earning respect by pleasing the people. Standing up the editor prepared to give the start signal for this event as the musicians created expectation with their intensifying interpretation of the circumstances.

The game was on and his opponent advanced swiftly and smoothly with his swords swinging in perfect unison creating a protective wall of deadly steel between himself and Benjobo. For an instant Benjobo admired his challenger with great respect. There was something different about this opponent, he could see why the crowd loved him, graceful, the man was swift and graceful. Reality quickly set in as one of his challenger's swords grazed his mail cuirass and cleanly sliced off a piece of his leather shoulder armor before glancing off the side of his helmet. Thankful for his heavy armor protection, he was concerned greatly with the speed of attack he just experienced by this challenging gladiator.

Benjobo and his adversary fought furiously for nearly ten minutes with the musicians interpreting their every move for the enthusiastic crowd. As his opponent connected solidly with Benjobo's shoulder armor, the impact spun them both around and Benjobo seized the opportunity to deliver a powerful upper body blow with the hilt of his sword. The shock drove his challenger into the sand and Benjobo spun around to complete his assault just as his opponent's sword connected with his heel, forcing his right foot high in the air.

Incredibly quick, Benjobo thought, I'm very fortunate to have superior armor, but the game is over, I'll finish this match before he can get up.

Catching his balance and planting his right foot firmly to launch forward for his final blow, extreme pain shot up Benjobo's leg and through his back. His opponent's sword had found its way between his foot armor and his padded leg armor and had damaged the Achilles tendon which snapped when he firmly planted his foot. Unable to use his right leg, Benjobo suddenly fell from victor to victim. Severely disabled, he collapsed on the sand. His challenger now stood over him clearly the conqueror and Benjobo's only hope was to drop his shield and remove his helmet in submission of defeat and hope for mercy from the crowd and the editor.

When Benjobo went down, the crowd began shouting, "He's had it."

Benjobo dropped his weapons and shield and submissively raised his left hand and index finger asking for mercy.

Quietly removing his helmet and looking up at the editor Benjobo gasped, "Jesus help me."

The editor was one of the disgruntled business owners that had lost their cargo when Shanesse was lightened in the storm and was very upset when Benjobo quickly sold himself to the lanista to avoid the trial. Now it was the editor's responsibility to decide the ending of the competition.

The crowd thoroughly enjoyed the performance and shouts of, "Let him go," could be heard as the people held their hands in the air with their thumb and forefinger pressed together.

The glimmer of hope quickly faded as multiple other merchants recognized Benjobo as the ship owner who sold himself to avoid trial. The crowd speedily followed their lead as they shouted, "Kill him," raising their thumbs in the air and turning them in towards their hearts. The editor raised his hand, stuck his thumb in the air and turned it towards his heart.

Honor was vital in the games and a gladiator was expected to die honorably. Getting up on his knees wrapping his arms around his opponent's thigh, Benjobo prepared for death in the gladiator way. His challenger took off his helmet and long flowing hair dropped to his shoulders. It wasn't a man at all it was an "Amazon." Women gladiators were known as Amazons. Benjobo suddenly knew why his opponent moved so differently. He had just been beaten and was going to die at the hand of a woman. She held his head with one hand and drove her sword through his neck. Benjobo felt warmth rush down over his chest and the noise from the crowd and the music from the musicians culminating frenzy all slowly quieted as the sun became dim and moved further and further away until it went black. He heard the mallet pounding and the flesh searing but he felt nothing.

A life was saved and freedom was won, the Amazon received her palm branch confirming another victory, and a laurel crown signifying an outstanding performance. Upon her returning from the victory lap around the arena, she was awarded a large sum of money and a wooden sword signifying that she would no longer have to risk her life in the games but was now a free woman. A woman of high social standing, having achieved what all gladiators strive for but few ever realize...wealth, freedom and honor. ☞

Chapter 19

A Powerful Tool

⚑

Climbing out of the skiff onto the dingy dock, Jag turned and took Jasmine's hand steadying her as she came ashore. Followed by ten other sailors including Captain Nassor, Capt. Warnken and Mecho, they made their way up to the street.

"Good to be home?" Nassor asked Jasmine.

"Malta is a great place to visit," Jasmine quickly responded, "but home is wherever you are Jag." Turning and looking at her husband with eyes of deep respect and tender love, she was very pleased that she had been so adamant with her father about not marrying one of those hollow diplomats that constantly filtered through Malta. "I knew when I married a sailor that home would be anywhere that we are together. And I plan to always be at home!" she said laughing. Turning to Captain Nassor she continued, "You wouldn't believe the difficulty I had escaping the clutches of some of those arrogant, smooth-talking diplomats that came blowing through Malta. I believe Daddy knew that most of them were a lot more interested in their political position with him than their interest in me. From little on up Daddy often told me that I'm not just a girl, I'm someone special and he would make sure I wasn't married off to someone simply to be their servant." Wrapping her arm around Jag, with a huge smile she proudly proclaimed, "I caught myself a real man."

"That you have," Captain Nassor assured her, "that you have."

"They don't come any better," Capt. Warnken said giving her a wink. Continuing he said, "I think Jag did rather well himself. You two definitely compliment each other."

Beaming with satisfaction at the high compliment from Capt. Warnken she said, "Daddy sure will be glad to see all of you." Just then the first coach pulled up, stepping back, pulling Jasmine with him Jag said, "After you gentlemen, we'll follow you in the next coach." Laughing quietly as they pulled away Jag said, "I recognized the coach driver."

Busting out laughing Jasmine said, "Yes, that was Wendell. They should have a very interesting ride to the estate."

The other four stood there with a look of bewilderment and Jag said, "Just ask them how their ride was when we get there. I'm sure they will have something to say about it, because they won't get to say anything from now until they reach Publius' estate."

"Is he a talker?" one of them asked.

Still laughing Jag said, "On my last visit I rode with him to Publius' place and only got about three words in edgewise even though he asked me questions. He never stops. I couldn't even answer the questions. He was still talking after he dropped me off! No one was in the coach, and he was still talking as he pulled away. What a guy."

The sky was a deep blue, the vegetation was lush and green and flowers of every bold island color were growing by the road.

"What an excellent day," Jasmine said as they arrived at her father's estate.

Coming over to the coach and reaching out his hand Publius cheerfully said, "Jasmine, It's so good to see you again."

Giving her daddy a big hug she said, "You must hear what awesome things our God has done."

Reaching out to shake his hand Jag was pleasantly surprised when Publius bypassed his hand and gave him a hug saying, "Welcome home my son."

As greetings were given all around, Captain Nassor made his way over to Jag. Standing by his friend he gently elbowed him and leaning close to his ear he said, "I take it you've met our friend Wendell before?"

Laughing quietly Jag whispered, "How was your ride?"

Captain Nassor was laughing also as he said, "That man can talk."

"I met him on my last visit," Jag said still laughing, "and I knew my words simply wouldn't describe the experience so I let you and Capt. Warnken experience the benefit of Wendell firsthand."

"I thought something was up when you so politely stepped back pulling Jasmine with you, and ever so bigheartedly allowed us to ride in the first coach," Captain Nassor said nodding his head.

Publius invited everyone to the garden where he had been entertaining some dignitaries earlier in the day. In the winter this beautifully landscaped garden looked grand but now during the growing season it was spectacular, with a variety of textures, shapes and patterns that took one's breath away. Peaceful and serene, it had become a preferred place for Publius to quiet his mind and meditate. Water flowed from natural springs creating a small stream which was directed by carefully fashioned stonework. Small ponds or lochans were situated on different levels connected by waterfalls which in turn created the soothing sounds of running water that was pleasantly accompanied by the distinct songs of the birds that called this paradise home. Ornamental plants and flowers from distant parts of the world complemented the stream. Paths meandered through the garden with strategically placed benches, some made of stone and some of wood. All were situated to best enjoy the stunning beauty, some in the bright sunshine with others shaded. Publius led his friends up a few steps in a long arc that were laid in stone, arriving at his favorite place in the whole garden. There was seating for ten or twelve persons by a quiet pool, shaded with a tightly woven thatch type roof supported by wooden columns, built purposely to blend well with the surroundings. Fish could be seen swimming in the pool and brightly colored birds came and went from the sculpted trees nearby.

As they were seated, servants quietly provided a refreshing blend of fruit juice and Publius addressed the group saying, "I wanted to bring you here to my favorite place in the garden. As I spend time meditating on the wonderful things our God has done for us here on Malta, I am astounded at how everything has changed. We have a history of worshipping many gods and goddesses. Our island is only nine miles long but we are one of the most strategic plots of land in the world. We have been influenced by many tribes and nations as they traveled through our land. We worshipped Baal, Nimrod, and many others, including ceremonial rituals to the goddess of Fertility with hypnotic dances and chants. We breathed the sweet narcotic smoke of burning sage and had powerful spiritual experiences. But our gods were challenged and beaten the day Paul, Ambassador of the One True God, came ashore. We worshipped Moloch and made human blood sacrifices to the gods of the underworld, represented by the serpent. The underworld gods, being severely threatened by the arrival of Paul, immediately retaliated with the deadly Naja haje bite. Paul, being a committed Ambassador of the One True God, even after the most grueling fourteen days of his life, showed no ill effects by the snake bite. Then as I'm sure you all remember, everyone on the entire island was healed. What an awesome God! Having dedicated our island to the One True God, we have experienced great things as our land has also been healed and restored."

Publius continued, "I have been having dreams and visions giving me insights into many things. When my daughter Jasmine came to me about Jag for example, I had peace in my heart about arranging her marriage with a sailor. During my meditation time right here in the garden, I began to piece the puzzle together. Jag had hidden certain facts very well for many years, but I suddenly realized who he was."

"How do you meditate without smoking sage and chanting?" asked Mecho. "I stopped meditating all together, not wanting anything to do with the false gods. I thought the ceremonial rituals and the hypnotic dance was something you had to do to get into meditation."

"No, quite to the contrary," Publius stated. "Meditation is actually a powerful tool of the believer. I purchased as many writings and historical documents of the faith as I could find. I recently acquired a copy of the torah from a group of Pharisees."

Breaking into the dialogue Captain Nassor asked with much amazement and surprise, "You purchased a copy of the Torah from a group of Pharisees? How did you do that!"

"It wasn't difficult," Publius said with a grin. "They are lovers of money. Show them the money and they will sell their own grandmother."

Everyone laughed and those who had any dealings with the Pharisees nodded an emphatic agreement with that statement.

"Bet it was expensive," the one sailor said. "I remember a group of them on our ship, carrying a torah. They acted like it was the most valuable thing on earth."

"They like the attention," Publius said. "With the slightest glimmer of gold, their values quickly adjust to fit the occasion."

"Tell us more about meditation," Capt. Warnken requested.

"About meditation," Publius continued, "I read of King David, a man after God's own heart spending time with his harp in the fields at night thinking on, or meditating on God and His Words. David's words are: 'May the meditation of my heart be pleasing in your sight, O Lord, my Rock and my Redeemer'. Another time he says: 'My mouth shall speak wisdom, and the meditation of my heart shall give understanding'. And Yet again: 'I have more understanding than all my teachers, for Your testimonies are my meditation'.

"I started noticing a parallel of great men of the faith, Moses, Joshua, Isaac and others. Their wisdom and insight was connected with their meditation time with the One True God. Their meditation seems to be a quiet time, clearing other invading thoughts from their minds and meditating on the things of God and His Truths, bringing their thinking into alignment with His thoughts. I personally find meditation to be very helpful in understanding the thoughts and intents of my Lord. My goal is to hear and act on His Words and not simply try to get His blessing on my plans."

"That sounds like a very noble goal," Capt. Warnken agreed. "How do you quiet yourself?" he asked.

"It takes practice; it's a learned discipline," Publius said. "Since you all have received a new life through Jesus and are believers in the One True God, would you like me to lead you in the basics right now?"

They all agreed.

Publius began with the basics, explaining how to settle the body down, starting with a comfortable sitting position. "Sit with your back straight and both feet flat on the ground," he said. For many of you, it will be directly off to sleep as we go through the different muscle groups, purposely relaxing the body. The fact is that these exercises are also very worthwhile after a long day of work; they will help you to relax and go off to sleep. But our goal right now is to relax your body and clear your mind so you can meditate on the One True God. Close your eyes gently, don't squeeze them tight. This shuts out the visual distractions that try to attract our attention. Next, place your hands on your legs, palms up. The hands are very sensitive and also cause distraction if they are in contact with your clothing. Take a deep breath and let it out, take another deep breath and relax as you let it escape. Take one more deep breath and let it out.

"Starting at the top of your head, relax the muscles at your scalp, feel the blood pulsing in your head. Next relax the muscles in your forehead. Allow the tautness to drift away. Now relax your face muscles around your eyes and mouth; it's ok if your jaw drops open a bit, simply relax.

"You must understand," Publius added, "the average person's mind wonders and thoughts flood in within just a few moments of quieting the body. I will have two of my musicians play softly as we continue."

Motioning to his two assistants who had arrived unnoticed and positioned themselves a short distance on either side of the small group, they began playing quietly.

"Now relax the muscles in your neck, and allow your shoulders to loosen. Concentrate on the chest area and the upper back, purposely relax these muscles. Notice your breathing and feel your heartbeat. Continue down to the abdomen and lower back, relax, relax."

Publius noticed that already four of the men were asleep. He smiled and continued, "Relax the hips and thigh areas and the muscles in the buttocks.

Continue down the legs and relax the knees and the calf muscles; now gently flex the ankle and foot muscles and allow them to completely relax."

"Completely relaxed, now remember you are in a safe place, quiet your mind and picture yourself sitting with Jesus and our Father, the One True God. Think on these words." Publius began quoting the writings of King David. (Ascribe or Give) [1] 'Ascribe to the Lord, O mighty ones, Ascribe to the Lord glory and strength. Ascribe to the Lord the glory due his name; worship the Lord in the splendor of his holiness. The voice of the Lord is over the waters; the God of glory thunders, the Lord thunders over the mighty waters. The voice of the Lord is powerful; the voice of the Lord is majestic.' [2] 'May the words of my mouth and the meditation of my heart be pleasing in your sight, O Lord, my Rock and my Redeemer.'

"Now quietly thank the Lord for all he has accomplished in your life. Don't bring Him questions. Thank Him for redeeming you; thank Him for this time that you can quietly sit with Him.

The music continued, and there was a very strong presence of the Lord most High in and among the group.

---

[1] Psalm 29:1-4 NIV
2 Psalm 19:14 NIV

Time passed, then Publius quietly continued, "Allow the Lord to speak into your life, no questions, just listen to His Words."
Twenty minutes seemed like only a moment and again Publius spoke, [1] 'I will praise the Lord, who counsels me; even at night my heart instructs me. I have set the Lord always before me. Because He is at my right hand, I will not be shaken.' [2] 'The Lord confides in those who fear him; he makes his covenant known to them.'

"Breath deep," Publius instructed. Then slowly continuing through each muscle group as he had earlier, he softly directed the men. "A few deep breaths, move your feet around gently, then flex the muscles in your legs and bend your knees. Moving up, flex the muscles in your upper legs and hips. Flex your back and again breath deeply. Move your shoulders around and stretch your neck. Now open your eyes and smile.

"How was your quiet time meditating on the words written about our Lord, thanking Him for all he's done for you? Did you meet with our Lord? Did He give you encouraging words?"

Tears streaming down Capt. Warnken's face he quietly said, "The Lord encouraged me in the words that Paul had prophesied back in Ostia. Paul said I would plant churches in places that I had visited as

---

[1] Psalm 16:7-8 NIV
[2] Psalm 25:14 NIV

Captain of Shanesse.   I am a very bold and courageous Captain, as capable as any, but I have been feeling extremely inadequate for the job of planting churches. In our meditation time, 'the Lord said He will never leave me nor forsake me. He will guide and direct as we plant churches. The church is His and He will cause it to prosper.' He has confirmed Paul's words and encouraged me greatly as I have set my goals to do exactly what He has requested."

With raised hands, Capt. Warnken thanked the Lord Jesus over and over. "With You all things are possible.   I can be successful promoting Your Kingdom, I can plant churches. Thank You Jesus!"

Jag spoke, "I was having a hard time with running a business for my family. I thought to properly promote the kingdom, I had to find a town and plant a church also. But the Lord has given me a great peace and confidence that I'm right where He wants me as I represent Him while working in the shipping business."

"Captain Nassor, you look like you had a good visit also," Publius observed.

"Yes, I was worried quite a lot about Francis. A marriage is being arranged for me but it is a full two years from now. I was very concerned about my responsibilities as captain, my safety, my future. All that having to line up as I do my best also to promote the Kingdom.   Actually I was very concerned that by some great uncontrollable turn of events, I would never see her again. I believe I could deal with that, but I could not imagine breaking her heart. Such a vibrant young lady, pure in heart, experienced salvation through Jesus at a young age, I have never seen such a gorgeous sparkle in someone's eye. She simply loves life!"

Jag walked over, gave Nassor a full strength sailor hug that would have crushed the average commoner, then with his hands on Nassor's shoulders, at arm's length looked him straight in the eyes and very knowingly said, "My friend, you're in love. Don't worry about all the details, two years will pass before you know it!"

"I had an excellent visit with Jesus, there certainly was a transfer of peace. I have confidence that everything is going to work out and I know that Jesus cares even more for Francis than I do."

By this time those who had slipped off to sleep, were very disappointed with themselves and had determined to practice this newly learned technique. Interestingly enough each individual, whether they fell asleep or not, recognized a difference within themselves and were fully convinced they encountered the One True God.

After a most excellent stay with Publius on the island, which seemed much too short, a huge entourage accompanied the group back to the docks to see them off. Jasmine had an additional wagon of her own with her share of supplementary valuables. Jag and his new bride discussed the necessity of some of her prized possessions being taken aboard the vessel. But as expected by all, Jasmine prevailed. After the skiff completed multiple trips transporting Jasmine's personal effects out to the ship, the group bid their farewells to their friends and family on Malta and boarded Pharos of the Sea.

"Weigh anchor," Captain Nassor ordered and the eager crew sprang into action. Within the hour they had harnessed the wind and Pharos of the Sea sailed gracefully out of the harbor enroute to Philippi.

Chapter 20

The Perfect Gift

An Easterly course took Pharos of the Sea towards Crete. It was difficult even to consider the reality of that being the same Adriatic Sea that Shanesse struggled through for fourteen grueling unrelenting days before her demise. Captain Nassor noticed Capt. Warnken standing by the stern rail one evening, gazing off in the distance enjoying a spectacular sunset.

Quietly joining him, Captain Nassor said, "What a difference a Nor'easter makes, eh?"

"I was considering that experience myself," Capt. Warnken responded. "I wouldn't wish it on my worst enemy. But it was worth it."

That statement took Captain Nassor by surprise. He tried not to picture himself and Pharos of the Sea facing a storm like that, but it had crossed his mind on numerous occasions. "How, what... really?" After a few moments of thought he continued. "I'm not sure I understand how that could be? I personally do my best to not think about that storm. Paul said to take every thought captive, and that has been helpful. If I meditate on that storm, fear still tries to come. As excellent as this ship is, I hope to never again face a storm like that." Then he added quietly, "Shanesse was a very capable vessel also."

"Nassor, my friend, surviving that big blow in itself would have certainly changed my life somewhat, but nothing I've ever imagined could change my life like meeting the One True God. I knew nothing of Jesus giving His life for us and being raised from the dead until I, a completely broken man, a captain without a ship, sat under Paul's teaching on Malta. Without the storm and the loss of my ship, I would never have taken the time to listen to the words of a prisoner whom I was transporting. My relationship with the Lord is worth the fourteen days of hopeless despair in the worst storm I've ever seen in my life and even the loss of Shanesse."

"Aye, Captain, you're very right about that. In my previous life, becoming captain of this vessel would have been the ultimate accomplishment."

"In your previous life?" Capt. Warnken asked with a puzzled look on his face.

"Yes, my previous life," Captain Nassor replied. "Paul explained, when we accept Jesus as our Lord, our old man dies and we are a new creation that never existed before. I agree with you Captain, it was worth the storm and worth losing Shanesse. Lives were spared on the beach, but I died right there alongside of you in Publius' meeting hall, where we both found new life in Jesus. It is, of course, a great honor to Captain this fine vessel, but Pharos of the Sea is merely a tool in the hand of a son, promoting his Father's kingdom. Light of the Sea, dedicated to the Savior Gods!"

At that, with a huge smile, Capt. Warnken broke out in song. His commanding voice was quickly accompanied by Captain Nassor and the crew who were working topside. The ship was engulfed with praises to the Savior Gods. Off duty sailors started emerging topside and joined the celebration. An accompanying echo could be heard as many of the passengers below sang along. Jag and Jasmine appeared having summoned those of their crew who played musical instruments and a magnificent impromptu concert of praise ensued.

The evening was warm, the sunset was breathtaking and Pharos of the Sea gracefully pressed forward, her prominent torch leading the way. The light of day faded but the worship intensified, drawing every soul aboard to the decks of the ship. The sounds of pure sweet worship surged out of the depths of every reborn spirit on the ship, creating an overwhelming flood of fervent love and gratitude that engulfed every individual occupying that small speck floating alone in the vast Adriatic sea which was being swallowed up by the night sky. The worship seemed to beckon the stars, first arriving one by one then by the hundreds followed by thousands until a glorious array filled the sky from horizon to horizon. The moonless sky was intensely stunning as one could see further and further into its depths, past the worlds, through the reaches of space and into the ages of time from where the master of the universe, the creator of all emerged. Accompanied by angels and accented by shooting stars that blazed through time arriving in the present, leaving trails of shimmering light, the Father Himself occupied the praise of the children He loved. The light of His being and His powerful presence clearly illuminated every intent of every heart. Tears streamed down faces in the majestic starlight. In time the songs faded but the voyagers remained motionless, sprawled out on the deck, some repenting profusely for past wrongs, others wanting the breathtaking experience to continue without end.

After the powerful evening of praise and worship, there were numerous passengers with many questions. Capt. Warnken started teaching each day after the evening meal. In a few days, most of the passengers and off duty sailors were regularly attending his meetings. The Word of the Lord proved powerful and effective as many lives were transformed, much like when Paul was teaching on Malta. Capt. Warnken himself was amazed. Without a doubt, it was not him. He was a commanding, powerful and confident captain who could single-handedly neutralize any person in the group, but he was very intimidated, standing up in front of this mixed group of men, women and even a few children, representing the One True God. Commanding a ship on the high seas with a group of hardened sailors and fighting off raiders in foreign ports of the world all seemed easy compared to this.

His knees felt weak and tears flowed easily, as he looked out over the faces, each one with a past of situations and choices that resulted in his or her present destiny. Some difficult, others fortunate, but each history included both right and wrong decisions. Capt. Warnken yearned to tell them that their destinies were not carved in stone! Looking out over this sea of situations and choices Capt. Warnken felt unqualified and overwhelmed. It was no easy task to teach them of the free gift, the free gift that one cannot buy no matter how vast his wealth nor can he earn no matter how vast his skills. This free gift will change a destiny forever, the free gift of life! The "Free Gift" that when accepted, "Will Cost You Everything." And having made "This Choice," one still has opportunities and choices!! Carrying the gift of life requires you to "Choose" to die to yourself daily!!! How do you explain that to these people? How do you explain that, for the one who gave His life to make this all possible? Capt. Warnken thought, this is much more challenging than captaining a shipload of the finest treasures through perilous seas with contrary winds, into savage ports of foreign lands! "That I can do!" he quipped aloud. Then he remembered the words of Jesus, "The burden is light and the yoke is easy." I have so much to learn, he thought. What am I doing here trying to teach these truths? With that, his mind went back to the praise and worship time the other night. The weightiness lifted; he smiled and knew he was not alone.

One evening after the meeting Captain Nassor found Capt. Warnken standing in the bow of the ship, both hands on the rail, looking quietly out over the water. "Captain, you certainly don't have to concern yourself about planting churches, you simply have it in you. You have a church going and you haven't even arrived at your destination."

"Yes, and what am I going to do with these people when we arrive?" Capt. Warnken asked. "That was never a concern for me before...they simply each went their own way, no longer any concern of mine." After a pause he continued, "I was questioning our Lord about what to do when I arrive in Philippi, I never even considered teaching along the way." After another pause, shifting his weight to the other leg, he turned and faced his friend who was also leaning on the rail with one hand and already looking at him. "My old job was much easier." He stated very matter of factly, smiling looking at Nassor and nodding his head.

"I was just thinking the same thing!" Captain Nassor observed, and they both enjoyed a good laugh which somehow seemed to bring things back into perspective. "Isn't it interesting how the Lord puts things in order? I don't suppose it's of any value worrying what you will do when you arrive.

It's easy to see the hand of God in action along the way. Surely He has a plan for Philippi also."

"Wouldn't it be great to see a bit more of the big picture on ahead?" Capt Warnken proposed. "I didn't know how things would go in court back in Ostia, but I very much could sense the Lord leading me one step at a time. Day by day I was able to focus on each necessary detail and by the time we had to appear in court, I had a mountain of paperwork perfectly in order without the help of Benjobo. Even today, that is completely amazing to me, but it sure would have been nice to know how it would all work out on ahead," he said, shaking his head recalling the intense pressure he felt during the long weeks of preparation for the court trial. "Another thing that's completely amazing to me is, in all my years at sea I've never seen such a close knit crew as you have. You operate this ship flawlessly as if they were simply an extension of your own hands! That my friend is commendable!"

"Let me say this, I too can see the Lord in every step of my journey," Captain Nassor agreed. "I was willing to do whatever the Lord asked, working with Paul, working with Beryl in his village, I was even willing to give up life at sea. The next thing I know, I'm captain of one of the finest vessels in the world, working for a good friend of mine who I never imagined could be a ship owner. On top of that, most of my crew accepted Jesus as their Lord and sat under Paul's teaching for three months and those that haven't are sitting under the very capable teacher Capt. Warnken, my best friend, right here on this voyage! How awesome is that?" He asked but quickly continued. "The Lord in our lives is the reason for the close knit crew you speak of, and He has also made you a very effective teacher, my friend."

The two friends stood quietly looking out over the water. After a few minutes of silent contemplation, Captain Nassor continued, "I'm not sure I want to see the big picture all at once. I would have had a very difficult time applying myself, as I helped Beryl if I knew this ship was waiting for me in Ostia. And having done my very best working with Beryl and teaching in his village, without distractions in the back of my mind about future responsibilities aboard this vessel, I ended up with an arranged marriage to a spectacular young lady who I can't stop thinking about. If I hadn't truly cared for Beryl and his needs, thinking only of sailing this ship as soon as I completed my time with him, I don't believe he would trust his daughter to me."

"You're so right," Capt Warnken agreed. "It would be hard to do our best here and now if we saw the big picture clearly, because we seem to assign the wrong value to some things." After a few moments of silence he continued, "On that note, I'll leave you to your thoughts, I need to get some rest."

Sailing to the north of Crete and maintaining a northeasterly course they carefully wove their way through numerous small islands, and began their turn North through the Aegean sea toward their destination.

Arriving in Neapolis, the port town for Philippi, the passengers had disembarked with many good-byes especially to Captain Warnken. His considerable time spent teaching the after dinner meetings had earned him much respect and many friends.

The work began as the cargo was off loaded onto ground transportation and prepared for the steep ascent into Philippi. This very prominent and wealthy city was known as 'The Gateway' connecting Europe and Asia. The Gateway was a strategically established garrison that controlled the Great Royal Route across Macedonia. This route known as the Via Egnatia, was a modern day road paved with stone and covered with hard sand. The heavily traveled road measured twenty feet wide and stretched nearly seven hundred miles; this road along with the port town of Neapolis had literally made Philippi a melting pot of culture. People and wares from the far reaches of the modern world could be found here. Pharos of the Sea had arrived with a full load of goods and many people, but the foremost reason for their visit to Philippi was the nearby Asyla gold mines. These mines had played a key role in helping King Philip II establish this strategic city and the more recently discovered Asyla mines were producing great wealth. Currently under the watchful eye of the Roman Empire, much of the gold and the coins produced by the onsite mint were shipped back to Rome. The documents for shipment were signed by Caesar himself. Pharos of the Sea was to transport a heavy load of gold bars and minted coins back to Ostia, enroute to Rome.

The gold shipment was delayed a few days, as it was to be highly secretive cargo that only a select few individuals knew about. The local officials in charge of the shipment wanted to wait until after the games had begun in the theatre, which would naturally divert most of the people's attention to the other side of the city. During this delay the crew had a few days to relax and Capt. Warnken took leave of the ship. Capt. Warnken said many good-byes, first to Captain Nassor and then to Jag and his new bride Jasmine. And then with a short encouraging speech to his longtime friends and faithful crew, he departed.

Capt. Warnken came to the address he was searching for. It was a well kept house attached to an exquisite retail shop. As he entered the shop he was met by a friendly young lady with an inviting smile in lovely apparel, trimmed in the finest of purple silk. She instructed him that it would be just a few minutes and encouraged him to have a seat by one of the small round tables. Disappearing into an adjacent room, she promptly returned offering him a warm beverage which Capt. Warnken graciously accepted, and she disappeared into another room. The shop was situated on the hilltop taking full advantage of the prevailing winds, allowing a soft breeze to carry just a hint of fine incense from deep within, throughout the rooms. The sun poured in strategically placed windows allocating the perfect lighting, accenting the stunning fabric displays. Warnken realized this was no ordinary shop. Towards the back was a highly refined middle aged woman negotiating with a man who appeared to be of significant social standing. Although the customer was arrogant and notably rather full of himself, it immediately became apparent that her negotiating skills, far exceeded his. Warnken marveled at her abilities as she completely dominated the negotiations but remained courteous and pleasant at all times, being careful not to damage her customer's fragile dignity. In a few minutes, an agreement was met and her customer left with a small parcel under his arm and a huge smile of satisfaction on his face. This was no ordinary lady either, he thought.

Capt. Warnken stood and asked, "Might you be Lydia?"

The lady turned and smiled as she gracefully walked in his direction. The light danced on her purple silk dress as it flowed and rippled in the breeze. Her royal attire accentuated her fluid movements. As she came up to him he could see a deep peace and contentedness in her eyes. Interesting he thought, I can see why people buy from her.

Reaching out her hand, "I am," she replied. "And who do I have the privilege of meeting here today?"

"I am Captain Warnken, but I bring you salutations from Paul the Apostle who is in Rome and doing well."

"Paul the Apostle," she repeated with a huge smile, and her face brightened even more. Motioning for him to sit down, she joined him and asked, "How is our friend Paul?"

Lydia summoned her young assistant and gave her some instructions. Before long a group of prayer warriors had gathered and the shop was closed. Lydia had excused herself for a few minutes and returned having changed clothing.

With her usual bright smile she explained, "I needed to get out of my work clothes." Warnken had a bit of a puzzled look so she continued, "It's much easier to sell purple silk if you wear it, don't tell them how good it looks, show them. But I don't wear it all the time. It makes some people uncomfortable when I dress like that, and it makes me uncomfortable if I accidentally mark or damage a dress." He smiled and nodded.

The afternoon turned into evening and the evening faded into night as time slipped by unnoticed. The locals spoke of Paul's time in Philippi and how his teaching changed their lives. They all listened, wide-eyed and astonished as Capt. Warnken relayed the events of the storm and losing his ship. He shared Paul's words from the Lord that proved true as they lost no lives and Paul himself survived the deadly Naja haje bite. He told them of Publius and the transformation on the Island of Malta and of Paul remaining a prisoner in Rome. Then he told of how Paul had requested that he visit Philippi and gave them the letter that Paul had written to their group. The letter encouraged them in the Lord and asked that they pray for him that he would present the gospel boldly and accurately to the Roman dignitaries and to the church in Rome. The letter also asked that they would receive Capt.

Warnken as they would receive him, and wished them all well as they continued in the faith.

Lydia's assistant invited them into another room where a magnificent meal awaited. They reclined at the tables, and the visiting continued as they took turns telling of what the Lord had done for them. Lydia's assistant told of how she had been a slave of some wicked men and Paul cast a spirit of divination out of her. She could not go on fortunetelling which in the past had earned her masters much money so they were going to kill her and have Paul and his assistant thrown into prison. Lydia bought her, saving her life and the Lord miraculously freed Paul and Silas from prison which in turn got the jailer and his whole family saved. It was late in the night when the people left for their homes and Lydia insisted that Capt. Warnken stay in the room they had prepared for Paul.

Later in the week, Capt. Warnken escorted Lydia and her assistant along with many other believers down to the ship as they wanted to meet the crew that Capt. Warnken told them so much about. After a grand tour of the elegant Pharos of the Sea, at Capt. Warnken's request, Lydia displayed samples of her fabrics to Jag and Jasmine along with Captain Nassor and a few of his officers. Much to her surprise and amazement, she took orders for nearly seven hundred thousand denarii worth of cloth. Jag ordered a full pound of purple silk for Jasmine and her family back home along with many other specialty materials and Captain Nassor ordered a large volume of upholstery fabric. Lydia was rather surprised but Capt. Warnken took her aside and explained that Jag was a part of the royal family of Alexandria, Jasmine was a part of the royal family of Malta and Captain Nassor was soon to marry the daughter of a fine craftsman who makes upholstered furniture for the dignitaries of Rome. Capt. Warnken offered to help Lydia arrange ground transportation to bring the cloth down to the ship. That was the only thing he was familiar with when it came to selling fabric. Lydia explained to Capt. Warnken that even though it was an excellent order, it wasn't that high of a volume and she could easily arrange its transportation down to the ship within a few days. The pure purple silk was the most difficult to get and it may take her some time to replace her stock, a pound of it sells for one hundred and fifty thousand denarii. The other material wasn't nearly that expensive as a pound of pure white silk for example sells for only twelve thousand denarii. Some of the upholstery material was rather expensive, it had pure gold threads woven into it. Capt. Warnken was amazed but said nothing. He had found years ago that even a fool appears wise if he keeps his mouth shut. He had never dealt in cloth but he knew his boots only cost two hundred and twenty denarii, and they were nice boots!

The secret cargo for Rome had continued quietly being loaded for a few days and the cloth from Lydia's shop arrived right on time. Within two weeks of her arrival, Pharos of the Sea again set sail on her return trip without Capt. Warnken. At their request, the church of Philippi was enjoying Capt. Warnken's teaching each evening for the next few weeks, as he awaited his connecting trip to Thessalonica. Capt. Warnken was, at Paul's request, planning to visit and encourage certain churches that Paul had established. ☚

Chapter 21

The Pirates, The Jewelry and "The Way"

꒰

Pharos of the Sea was scheduled for one quick stop in the Cayster River Harbor of Ephesus, one of the greatest seaports in the world. She was slated to pick up some dignitaries in Ephesus then on to Ostia. Rarely did any significant ship sail by without at least a quick stop to pickup or drop off passengers or wares. Ephesus' colorful culture came from far-reaching influences over land and sea. Three major roads led to the coastal city, one from Babylon, one from Smyrna and one from the Meander Valley, all converging on the harbor.

Pharos of the Sea lay elegantly at anchor in the busy Cayster River Harbor. Skiffs traveled back and forth bringing her high-ranking passengers and their belongings aboard. Jag and Jasmine welcomed their guests and deck hands showed them to their quarters. Captain Nassor, quietly and unnoticed, strategically placed the crew on high alert with weapons out of sight but within easy reach. Their rigorous training and experience in these situations gave onlookers and passengers a relaxed sense of tranquility, as sailors from the deck to high in the rigging seemed to be enjoying the view: mending sails, swabbing the deck, chatting by the rail, but all were keenly alert. Pharos of the Sea laid low in the water clearly telling any seasoned sailor her cargo hold was already to capacity. With passengers coming aboard, it was undoubtedly no secret on the docks that she came from Philippi and was bound for Rome. A savvy band of rogues with only a small imagination would have a wholehearted interest in a large elegant vessel loaded in Philippi, bound for Rome! The small sturdy wooden boxes deep in her holds were supposed to be a secret.

The passengers were brought aboard promptly with the entire crew praying that the fair winds would continue long enough to sail out of the harbor with no delay.

Mecho made his way over to Nassor. "Captain, I don't like the looks of this vessel coming our way. She was laying at the dock and took on a full load of men, definitely with an agenda, and not your average passengers wandering around familiarizing themselves with the vessel."

"Yes, I saw that, look how high she's riding in the water."

"High and fast," Mecho observed. "I don't like it Captain. She's coming too close, there's no reason to come our way, she should stay higher on the wind to exit the harbor without having to tack."

At that moment the last of the passengers were coming aboard. Six of them, or better stated, one last passenger with five personal assistants. A big mouth and a bad attitude immediately became apparent as he argued vigorously with Jag and Jasmine.

"Mecho, keep an eye on that vessel," Nassor said. "I'm going to check on this obnoxious idiot."

Walking amidships, Captain Nassor confirmed that his crew were noticing the coming vessel and not distracted with the irate passenger.

Walking up to the group Nassor asked, "Is everything alright?"

Jag motioned to the disruptive man and said, "This is Metri."

Metri, the leader of the small group acknowledged Captain Nassor's presence with a barrage of curses and swearing. Captain Nassor walked right up to him, and in a very authoritative voice said, "I am Captain of this vessel, what can I do for you and your friends today?"

Metri never missed a beat, his face now all red with the veins bulging in his neck demanded that he be given the royal treatment that he deserved.

Glancing in the direction of the suspicious vessel, Captain Nassor noticed that it was now sailing straight towards them, and closing.

"Look at me when I'm talking to you!" Metri bellowed, and turned on Captain like a rabid bear.

The second he laid a hand on the captain, three of his five attendants produced weapons in an aggressive show of force. Instantly, with one sweep from the captain whose patience had just run out, the aggressive man found his own feet high above his head and he seemed to hover there in his fine robes for just a second, as the captain made contact with the closest weapon handler. Then gravity took over as Metri's disoriented frame came crashing to the deck with his entire weight driving his face into the planking. Simultaneously Jag had disarmed a second aggressor and turned to deal with the third only to find him wincing in pain as another crew member held his own dagger to his throat. Four of the crew had already arrived to assist if necessary and the other two attendants of the disabled man wisely backed off in submission.

With their latest passenger out cold sprawled on the deck in a disarray of fine robes and bleeding profusely from his broken nose, Captain Nassor glanced at Jag who now had control of the three aggressive attendants and he nodded towards the more pressing issue. The closing vessel was disturbingly near and Captain gave the signal for his crew to hold as everyone prepared for the imminent attack. The approaching vessel suddenly changed course and sailed by a mere thirty meters away. There were far too many men on their deck to be a legitimate vessel and they were trying diligently to look nonchalant as they closely surveyed Pharos of the Sea and her crew.

Captain's orders rang out. "Haul the anchor." And the crew sprang into action. Mecho already by his side, Captain Nassor asked without changing his gaze in the direction of the departing vessel. "How many do you figure?"

"A good two hundred boarded at the dock about half of them appear to be on deck. Their regimented appearance would make them a highly trained group of mercenaries in my opinion. They're not provisioned for weeks at sea. They had few water barrels on deck and they're riding very high in the water. She's not loaded with cargo."

"High and fast," Captain Nassor said confirming Mecho's words from earlier. "They looked exceptionally malicious; I was concerned they may ram us. They were flying too much sail for boarding without severe damage. The sooner we get out of this harbor, the better I'll feel. I want some sea room to maneuver. Keep an eye on that vessel, long as you can see her, I want to know where she goes.

Shouting orders, Captain Nassor continued. "Secure the skiff on the double! Underway without delay! I want speed! Fly everything we have the moment the anchor breaks free! Two Seven Zero as soon as we have steerage! Move, Move, Move!"

Nassor was joined by Jag who asked. "What's up with that vessel that was checking us out?"

"I'm very concerned about her; she's up to trouble. Close as Mecho and I can figure, she's filled with pirates. She already left the harbor and turned south out of sight"

"Not good," Jag replied very seriously. "When we get some sea room and some clean air outside this harbor, you think we can out run her?"

"Not likely, she's running high in the water, light and fast. I'm guessing that she has about two hundred armed men aboard with only one thing in mind. She's not provisioned for open sea. My guess is she's going to lay out there behind one of those small islands and try to intercept us. We'll fly everything we got but we are running heavy."

"Yes, I know it," Jag said. "And I believe it's their intention to lighten our load. You suppose

Philippi had a security leak? I purposely didn't allow any passengers to book from Philippi to Ephesus to avoid any unnecessary exchange of information. No one from our vessel, with the exception of our skiff crew, was ashore.

Captain Nassor smiled, looked him in the eye and said, "Our port authority papers list us as having come from Philippi and going to Ostia. We arrive laying low in the water and take on a few wealthy individuals enroute to Rome."

"Doesn't really take a scholar to figure out what we're carrying does it? God be with us," Jag commented, then continued. "We will be out of the harbor well before sunset, that's certainly a plus. And we are a very fast vessel, but we're heavy."

Pharos of the Sea smoothly moved forward as her sails captured the wind. The skiff was aboard and those weighing the anchor struggled to complete the job as they still had about sixty feet of chain and anchor to retrieve. Mecho was on the wheel skillfully bringing her to two hundred seventy degrees, on course to depart Cayster River Harbor as promptly as possible.

The afternoon was extraordinary, blue skies with a soft wind and high wisps of white clouds far above the tallest mast. An immense rig filled with white sails towering above an elegant vessel, gracefully pressing through turquoise waters toward the open sea. The passengers who started emerging onto the deck had no hint of the intense situation but stood amazed at the beauty of the moment.

Jasmine joined her husband and asked, "By the way Captain, what do you think of that arrogant group of self proclaimed heroes that came aboard?"

Captain Nassor shook his head and said, "Someone like that is trouble enough but his timing was really off. He picked the worst possible time to threaten us. Ship and crew are within moments of a life or death skirmish and he's threatening physical harm to the owner and lays hands on the Captain. Foolish, very foolish; I hope I wasn't too brutal with him, is he ok?"

"He's fine," Jasmine said. "He woke up on the way to the brig; he will have three days to consider his ways, before he and his three bodyguards are free men again."

Jag interjected, "It's been a few years since I've met someone that full of himself. The whole problem started with an accidental splash he received getting out of the skiff. Then our attendant went to help him aboard by taking his precious bag that he was struggling with and he went crazy. Thanks for your assistance."

"Where are the other two bodyguards?" Captain Nassor asked.

Jasmine replied, "They seemed to lose all interest in fighting when they saw how promptly the others were neutralized. They are currently occupying one of our finer quarters, alone. It had been reserved for our unruly friend with his five 'attendants.'"

Jag chimed in, "I hope they learned something. They best tread softly for the remainder of this trip. I don't trust them; they have that wild look in their eyes. The whole gang of them seems to think they are well above all other human beings."

Exiting the harbor with another nautical mile to the open sea, all eyes were scanning the horizon for signs of the rebel ship. "She's gone sir," was the report that kept coming to Captain Nassor.

"She's hiding," was his reply.

Suddenly a call rang out from high in the rigging. "Vessel at eleven-o-clock." The passengers did not think a thing of it as there were numerous vessels coming and going. The vessel in question came in view from the deck a few minutes later. She was laying behind a small island, hove to. When a sailing vessel heaves to, she keeps her sails up but maneuvers the vessel into position where the wind and the sails work against the rudder and keel angles which in turn allows her to remain fairly stationary. She can be underway rather quickly compared to lowering the sails and anchoring.

As expected, she turned and was quickly underway setting a course to intercept Pharos of the Sea. The breeze had stiffened slightly as they departed the harbor and the clean air passing over the sea, in comparison to the agitated and swirling air that passed over the land, also gave them added speed. Captain Nassor ordered that they hold course. It now appeared that their paths would cross about four nautical miles ahead or within about an hour's time at their current speed. The passengers continued to enjoy the view as they quietly departed the great seaport. To them it was simply a spectacular day to be on the water.

Half an hour passed and there was some concern arising among the passengers as it became apparent the two vessels were on intersecting paths. Captain Nassor made the announcement that there was question as to the intent of the approaching ship, and the passengers were ordered below. The crew stood ready but the order remained to keep their weapons hidden. The captain on the pirate ship was apparently very capable of handling his vessel. He carried significantly more speed being so high in the water and his timing was impeccable. At only twenty yards separation, their intentions were stated loud and clear, "Heave to and we will spare your lives." Their deck was literally crowded with armed soldiers of fortune eager to do battle.

Most of the passengers had locked themselves in their quarters, but Jasmine was below with that small group of believers, entreating God in Jesus' name. They all prayed quietly with some taking turns leading aloud.

Jasmine prayed, "Father we live in the secret place of your presence. You are the Most High God; we dwell in safety under Your shadow, Almighty God. Mighty Warrior, King of kings, You are our Lord, our fortress, our refuge. It is in you that we put our trust. We refuse fear, fear has no place on this vessel, fear has no place among our crew. We shall be bold, we shall be strong because You Lord, our God are with us. Hundreds may fall on the pirate ship, but it will not destroy us. With our eyes we will look and see the reward of the wicked. We have made you Lord our dwelling place. You have placed angels in charge over us to keep us in all our ways. We call on you now in this time of trouble, deliver us, honor us, show us your salvation! A loud crash and splintering of timbers was heard as Pharos of the Sea shuddered and jolted.

Topside was intense; staunch arrogance and passionate greed emanated off the approaching vessel and her iron-faced men. The pirate ship easily closed within casting distance and the enemy stood ready with grappling hooks.

"Hard to starboard! Evasive! Evasive! Evasive!" Captain Nassor shouted.

Evasive repeated three times was a code word developed by Captain Nassor for his crew in situations like this. It simply meant, turn hard away from the aggressor with an immediate turn hard into the aggressor. In the turn hard away, the crew stationed on the rail would cut the rope lashings holding four sets of defenders upright and they would drop down into horizontal defense position. Defenders were sets of sharp metal spikes hinged solidly on the hull and stowed upright and unnoticed into the ship's railing. It actually looked like heavy metal railing supports in the upright position. But in the down position, heavy metal shafts protruded aggressively toward the opposing vessel with razor sharp spear-shaped heads. The defenders were supported against the ship's superstructure and internally heavy timber reinforcement beams strengthened the impact area. With the weight of a ship behind them, they would drive through heavy planking.

The same maneuver included a dozen sharp shooters with bows to neutralize specific targets in the transition time between the starboard turn and the opposing port turn as the ship steadied momentarily. The targets were the man on the wheel, the captain and his officers.

Pharos of the Sea was longer with much taller masts than the pirate ship. The pirate ship's captain had just ordered his men to cast their grappling hooks and reel her in. Someone on Pharos of the Sea scrambled to release one of the hooks, acting in amazing inexperience and promptly got himself tangled in the attached line. A second man ran to his aid and foolishly positioned himself between the entanglement and the railing trying to assist. The 'hard to starboard, evasive, evasive, evasive' order had already gone out. Pharos of the Sea reacted smoothly turning to starboard. This tensioned the grappling lines and the two inexperienced seaman were snatched over the rail. The aggressor ship followed abruptly turning to starboard. Simultaneously the crew dropped the defenders and Pharos of the Sea turned hard into the approaching vessel. During the transition moments, the enemy captain took an arrow in the eye and two in the chest, the man on the wheel took one in the shoulder, one in his side and one cleanly in his ear. Two other men dressed as officers also had been disabled by the marksmen. With no one on the wheel to react, the aggressor vessel crashed forcefully into the protruding defenders which effectively pierced her hull. The destruction was greatly amplified by the added wave action of the sea, leaving a wake of twisted splintered and mangled planking tangled in lines and rigging.

Suddenly fire broke out and black smoke bellowed skyward. The pirate ship had fire pots with hot coals and flasks of oil setting by her rails with the intention of starting multiple small fires aboard the distressed vessel. The fires were not to sink their captured prize but to divert many of the crew's attention from the fight to extinguish the fires.   The plan severely backfired as the heavy metal defender shafts pierced the hull and splintered the decking, breaking many of the flasks of oil and shattering two of the firepots.   Hot coals with showers of sparks rolled across the splintered deck igniting the spilled oil from the broken flasks. Burning violently, liquid fire flowed across the deck and down inside their ship through the broken planking.

Nassor's men fought furiously with the pirates coming aboard and struggled to cut free of the burning vessel.   Having turned back hard to starboard after the impact in an effort to dislodge the defender spikes, the wind was directly behind them but they were in great danger of the fire spreading to their ship.   Continuing their starboard turn, placed the burning ship to leeward and within moments she was cut free of her restraining lines.

"Give us some sea room!   Check for fire!" Captain Nassor ordered as they sailed away from the burning wreck. "Face down or die!" The order reverberated and was repeated by all the officers.

Vastly outnumbered the fighting intruders quickly obeyed. Only forty two men had managed to come aboard Pharos of the Sea, as great pandemonium had erupted aboard their vessel with no captain, wheelman or commanding officers and a fierce fire burning out of control. It was confirmed that Pharos of the Sea had no fire, just a scorched railing and some damaged defender shafts. One set had been torn completely off and remained imbedded in the enemy ship and one set was damaged beyond repair. The other two sets could be repaired and reset into their hiding positions.

"Bring her about," Captain Nassor ordered. "That ship isn't going to survive, she was ablaze from deep within. I saw men who had oil spilled on them and were ablaze jumping in the water as we were departing, we need to check if any of them are still alive. Prepare the skiff on the double. Daylight is fading fast."

A quick count left twenty of the enemy dead aboard Pharos of the Sea with six seriously wounded and sixteen firmly lashed together awaiting their fate. With great relief all the crew were accounted for. There were multiple flesh wounds but nothing life threatening. A sailor brought some bad news about the two men he saw snatched overboard entangled in the grappling line. Quickly another count was made. All the crew were accounted for. Nassor questioned the crew, had anyone else witnessed the two men go overboard? Three sailors had seen it happen, but no one recognized the victims. The witnesses did report that the two victims were certainly not familiar with working lines on a ship. They did everything wrong, the first victim stepping into a coil of rope and the second one trying to free him was standing on the tension side of the problem. A complete lack of experience at sea was the real killer, the mishap was clearly avoidable. Four men were sent to count the passengers.

The passengers had been ordered below well before the skirmish for their own safety but Captain Nassor had a good idea who did not obey. He sent Mecho directly to Metri's quarters, knowing that he and three of his attendants were definitely below as they were occupying the brig, but he suspected the other two were the victims.

Jasmine made her way topside as soon as she was informed the skirmish was over. The others were worshipping God and giving Him thanks for their protection. She was attending to the wounded and praying for each of them.

It was quickly confirmed that the two victims were Metri's bodyguards, and Captain Nassor went to inform him of his loss. Upon Captain's arrival, Metri began cursing loudly, demanding to know what they ran into and who was the incompetent fool on the wheel, followed by another venomous barrage of obscenities.

Captain Nassor was very straightforward and to the point. "We were attacked by pirates. All passengers were ordered below but your two attendants ignored orders and paid for their mistake with their lives. I am truly sorry for your loss and the loss of life."

Metri let loose with another round of obscenities, cursing the men that died, their parents, their relatives and ultimately cursing God. What a decrepit man, Nassor thought as he left the cell. He's having trouble even living with himself. You couldn't pay me enough to be his bodyguard.

After an exhaustive search well into the night, the fire had claimed the other vessel and it sank beneath the surface. In all they retrieved another twelve men from the sea. With the skiff back aboard and secured, and the surviving attackers well cared for but confined in special quarters they again set their course for Ostia. The crew was exhausted and all but the necessary few required to sail the vessel on a calm night, resigned to their quarters. What a day!

The days that followed saw a great increase in those who were genuinely interested in Mecho's evening teaching sessions. Although the wealthy individuals proved very difficult to teach the ways of the Lord, they attended the meetings because of the fear they experienced when they were under attack. Everyone knew that the pirates would have simply killed them and confiscated their goods. But most were not ready to face death. However, they were terribly guarded with their own true lives and feelings. They were accustomed to living a make-believe life with pasted on smiles and doing exactly what was expected of every wealthy individual. Going to the right parties, visiting the right people and acting like you're supposed to. Nevertheless to accept a free gift from a God they could not see was proving to be a difficult process for some, as their whole lives had been built on their intellect, and they simply could not wrap their minds around this teaching. It was only available by faith. When they finally humbled themselves and accepted this challenging teaching of faith, wow what an impact. It completed what they had been secretly searching for. A free gift that was too big, too powerful, too awesome, too incredible, too fulfilling for words to describe it and too valuable for money to buy it. It was a life-altering step into a different realm. It was what they were searching for in the temples of their false gods, in their quest for wealth and fame, in their search for status and glory. It was a transformation, a metamorphosis that simply could not be explained, it had to be lived.

One evening the exceptionally belligerent Metri and his three attendants decided to grace the evening meeting with their presence. The moment he realized the meeting was all about God, His Son Jesus and the way of the Lord, Metri exploded in his usual barrage of curses and stormed out with his attendants in tow. As much as he despised Captain Nassor, who he cursed every time he looked after his broken nose, he diligently searched him out to place a formal complaint about the onboard meetings promoting 'The Way'.

In a dramatic display of emotion, Metri went into much detail explaining to Captain Nassor how dangerous and destructive this foreign doctrine called 'The Way' really was and that he actually found that it was being promoted on this very vessel!

After patiently listening to Metri's extended version of how dreadful and destructive this religious practice was, Captain Nassor politely said, "Yes, I'm very familiar with The Way, I am a believer in Christ Jesus, and it would truly do you good to look into it further."

In an amazing exhibit of highly developed foolishness, Metri exploded into a fit of rage and cursing loudly he turned to take hold of Captain Nassor. Catching himself, he thought better of it and instinctively put his hand to his swollen nose. Storming off Metri was shouting about going to the top as he departed on a mission to find the owner of the vessel.

Having no success with Jag and Jasmine, but finding with much dismay they too were believers, Metri went about quietly trying to get the crew in an uproar about this destructive belief. It seemed that every crew member he spoke with ended up being committed to 'The Way'. This news was most distressing to Metri and he hid himself away, secluded in his quarters most of the time for the remainder of the trip.

As Pharos of the Sea pressed on toward Ostia, they passed through a frontal system and the weather deteriorated rapidly. The crew secured the vessel for rough seas and the passengers were confined to their quarters. With all but the storm sails stowed, Pharos of the Sea negotiated the frontal system with little difficulty. She rolled considerably with quartering seas off her stern making life below decks difficult for her passengers but of little concern for the crew. Imbedded thunderstorms within the weather system created strong gusts and a few particularly close lightning strikes were followed by incredibly loud reports of thunder that reverberated through the vessel.

Her decks were not awash and the storms were short lived as Pharos of the Sea emerged out of the frontal system with no difficulty. Notably cooler temperatures accompanied clear skies as the passengers again graced the decks but Captain

Nassor remained below having responded to a distress call.

One of Metri's attendants had arrived in a panic during the storms and requested the ship's doctor who knowing the previous problems, refused to enter Metri's quarters alone. Captain Nassor offered his assistance. Metri suffered from seasickness and having taken multiple doses of his personal physician's seasickness remedy, he was distraught, screaming that he was going to die. Captain Nassor along with the ship's physician had arrived promptly and talked gently with Metri, calming him down. It was like opening a book and reading about Metri's life. Any question that Captain asked, Metri answered with no hesitation or reserve. Having retrieved the bottle of medication, the doctor read the label. The distressed attendant made it clear that the bottle was unopened when Metri fell ill a few hours ago, now only half remained. The doctor explained that Henbane with scopolamine was very effective for seasickness but Metri already had far exceeded the proper dosage. He said there should be no long lasting effects, but do not allow Metri to have any more, as it is he will sleep a lot for the next few days and remember nothing.

Captain Nassor sat quietly as the heavily sedated man told his story.

"I was a prosperous businessman in Ephesus and things were going well. Ephesus being a trade center for the world and situated in a very fertile valley made life good for all. And most importantly Ephesus is the home of Artemis, daughter of Zeus and Leto, twin sister of Apollo. Artemis, the goddess of fertility has the largest temple in the world located right in Ephesus. I was the well known 'Demetrius, Master Craftsman.' I made tribute statues of Artemis, also know as Diana to the Romans.

"A destructive cult was introduced to our great city and their followers spoke against Artemis. The cult praised another god and his son Jesus and taught people 'The Way' which denounces the great virgin goddess Artemis. They spoke of mighty things and of their Jesus being a healer. I stood strong against the cult, knowing that Artemis and her brother Apollo bring divine healing.

"My efforts failed to drive out 'The Way' and Artemis suffered greatly as many of our own people not only stopped buying her statues but started destroying the ones they had. The great virgin goddess Artemis is also known for bringing sudden death to women and spreading leprosy, rabies and gout to those with whom she is displeased. My wife got leprosy and my daughter who cared for her mother while she was sick, died suddenly. I realized how I failed Artemis and that's why my family had to die. A few months later my dog died from rabies, and I suffer with the gout.

"Since then I have poured my life into my work and advanced from silversmith to goldsmith and precious stones. I worked my way to the top and received an order for two sets of matching jewelry for the royal family in Rome. This was my opportunity of a lifetime, a chance to re-establish myself after so much misfortune. I worked diligently and completed the one set and had just a few months of work to complete the second. I shipped the first set of jewelry on one of the finest vessels available; she even carried the Gold Seal of Caesar. Months later I learned she went down in a storm and all the cargo was lost. I'm carrying the second with me," he said as he produced an incredibly detailed wooden block from the personal bag he was carrying. It had intricate carvings and very unusual grain patterns and was inlaid with ivory designs, accented with precious stones in gold settings. Wide eyed, Captain Nassor immediately recognized the masterpiece. It was identical in every way to the one he regrettably threw into the sea while struggling to save Shanesse. As Metri handled it, the whole top lifted to one side on hidden hinges. Inside, perfectly fitted and formed, nestled in a layer of fine cloth was a second set of the finest pieces of jewelry Captain Nassor had ever seen. As Nassor took a closer look Metri protectively pulled it away closing the box and returned it into his bag explaining, "I personally am delivering this set to Rome.

"I don't know what more to do for Artemis, I don't know why she stays so angry with me? I gave her huge gifts and worshipped many hours in her temple. But Artemis' twin brother Apollo, who brings sudden death to men, already claimed the lives of two of my assistants. And now the storm, I thought the ship was going down today, taking me and this last set of jewelry with her. I have sold my business in Ephesus and hired five assistants to accompany me to Rome to deliver my jewelry. I have no family remaining in Ephesus and this is my last big chance to make a name for myself." Leaning back on his couch with tears streaming down his cheeks, the huge dose of medication that had successfully allowed him to bare his soul promptly ushered him off to sleep.

Captain Nassor wanted desperately to share 'The Way' with him and see him set free but for the time being, he was gone. The drug induced sleep had overcome him and it would be many hours until he was again his arrogant miserable self. ☞

Help us bring new life and excitement to familiar events in history.

We know that word of mouth is a very powerful promotion for this book. Share how it has challenged or encouraged you. Discuss it with others on Face Book, Twitter and your personal blog space but don't reveal the plot, encourage them to read the book themselves. Consider giving a book as a gift to your friends and acquaintances or even to strangers, it will introduce them to powerful kingdom concepts. Make it available in your church bookstore.

Consider writing a book review for your local paper or website.

Ask friends who are public speakers, authors, pastors or business persons to review the book and post their comments in their newsletters and websites.

Thank You, We Sincerely Appreciate Your Assistance,
Captain Clair - for the entire Refreshing Leaders Team

Visit us at:
www.RefreshingLeaders.com
Contact Information:
captainclair@refreshingleaders.com
1-877-732-2278

Discount prices are available for resale. Consider a book display at your place of business.

Contact us for information concerning having the author speak at your event or to your organization.

Printed in the United States
219050BV00001B/2/P